Pedwyn Dale

Pedwyn Dale

Donald Lee Sadler

Illustrations by Mark Wayne Russell

For Magdalena:

who once believed the Faerie tales her father told her

ISBN: 979-8-35093-219-5

"Forgetfulness is a form of freedom."

--Kahlil Gibran

1

Tad Tucker crawled into the back of his parents' blue station wagon with a sour look. He absentmindedly pushed aside his younger sister Erin, causing her to cry out. His father started yelling about the shoving of his sister and something about the mud he was tracking all over the seat, but Tad was not listening. He did not care to hear anything at that point in time. Tad had blown it. He had given up the game winning goal. He had let his teammates and his coach down. He had lost the game. What Tad needed now was for fathers and little sisters to leave him alone. The rain that had begun to fall almost as soon as the ball went through the net continued to beat against the window. He could still see himself diving for the shot, coming up just short as it caught the inside pole and bounced in for the defeat.

"Good try, son," his father said trying to console him and only making matters worse. Tad stared out the car window and wondered how he could fake sick on Monday. School would be a nightmare after such humiliation. Because, not only had he given up the game winning goal, but Patty Greene saw it happen. Patty Greene was just about perfect in Tad's eyes, and if her witnessing his folly was not bad enough, the goal was scored by Chuck Bain. Chuck Bain, the biggest, ugliest, meanest, bully in the fourth grade. Southern Shores Middle School had been haunted by his unbearable ilk for too long now. Tad could count on his personal haunting to continue for the remainder of

9

the school year. In time he might have learned to live with losing a soccer game, but Chuck Bain would make it almost impossible to forget. That save would have spoken wonders for Tad and his friends who were the object of Bain's one-buffoon crusade to humiliate them in front of the whole school. His classmates did not care who was smarter. Academic achievement was not high on the list for popularity in the fourth grade. Being able to beat up every kid in the school, as Bain could, was however a most enviable trait. Lunch money would continue to be stolen, food would continue to be taken, arms would still be twisted, noogies and swirlies in abundance; life was still going to be a series of trying to avoid Chuck Bain in the hallways, and all because of one lousy goal. Monday was not going to be fun.

His parents drove on unaware of his personal pain. His sister also seemed unconcerned, more content to braid Barbie's hair. Tad rolled his eyes and hoped the rain would let up. He needed a long bike ride to take his mind off this tragedy.

"How about a nice-try milkshake, Tiger?" his dad was still trying to comfort.

Tad rolled his eyes again.

"He doesn't want a milkshake, Ronald; now would you please get us home", said his mother. She had not spoken all day to his father and the look she got from the driver confirmed Tad's suspicion; something was wrong with his parents. He might have only been ten years old, but he knew enough to know when things were out of place. His parents hardly spoke anymore, and his dad always had an excuse to miss dinner. He wondered what would happen if they decided to divorce. Would he have to decide who he wanted to live with? And what about Erin? Sure she grated his nerves, but she was still his little sister and he admitted to himself he would miss her if they were separated. He tried to stop thinking these things and his thoughts returned to the depression of the game. The storm continued to rage, and Tad could not remember a more violent rain. Fitting end to a wonderful day he thought.

His parents continued to look forward, both acting as if the other were absent. Erin had fallen asleep with her doll in her lap, so Tad continued to stare out the rain-soaked window.

So it was, that through the uncomfortable silence hanging inside the car like a shroud, despite the constant whir of the windscreen wipers as they fought the oncoming downpour, Tad Tucker first laid eyes on Pedwyn Dale.

2

Pedwyn Dale awoke earlier that particular morning and rose out of bed. His legs were stiff with the reminder of a restless sleep, dreaming of things he could now barely remember, and a feeling of uneasiness was upon him, for his dreams were of dark things. He did not bother putting on his hat or shoes since he had fallen asleep with them both still on - and it truth, nearly always did. Yawning, he stretched weary muscles, vigorously shook his head to ease the ringing in his ears, adjusted his woolen red hat, and professed himself fully awake and ready for work. A quick easy breakfast of eggs and milk was consumed with only minimal amounts ending up in his whiskers and upon his worn shirt. He searched around his tiny house until he found his bucket and with a skip, he was out the door. He whistled down his walk so none of the neighbors would ever assume he was not having the most perfect of mornings.

"Ahh tis a fine new day, Mr. Dale" he said, - this being how he referred to himself. "A fine new day indeed" he repeated. Pedwyn Dale stood about a foot and a half tall. He rather resembled a wiry old man who was very thin considering the amount he often ate. His hat was worn and probably once a much brighter red than its current hue. Tight skin wrapped around his wise little eyes and overly large nose. His mouth was almost invisible behind his dull grayish-brown whiskers and hanging beard. He wore a dingy white shirt underneath a hole-infested green overcoat, whose tails were torn to the point that one was much longer than the other. Knobby knees peeked out from holes in his dark brown knickers, and his uniform completed itself with tidy black shoes whose brass buckles were worn and chipping. There were much better-dressed Fae in his neighborhood and village, and there were some who barely bothered to dress at all, but Pedwyn Dale was content with his appearance. He once explained to a snobbish Sprite neighbor that his wardrobe was "comfortable and true" to his lifestyle. The snooty Sprite merely smiled, but then gossiped to all that would listen how their strange neighbor was a bit odd. Sprites simply cannot abide unpolished buckles.

Pedwyn Dale swung his bucket along the same path as he did every day to work. The well-worn trail led through the sweet fields and glens of Hollow Hill, past waving folks, and those who peered behind closed windows. Sometimes young Pixen skipped alongside him trying to trick him into a song, and more often than not Pedwyn Dale laughed and played their games. Occasionally, he would pass a friend and stop to talk for longer than he should, having to work longer into the day to fill his buckets. Pedwyn Dale picked elderberries. This job held prestige with the Faeries. For you see, elderberries were not only one of the more desired forms of revelry amongst the Wee Folk, but they were also in fact the hardest to come by. Elderberry bushes only grew in the Mists between our world and the world of Faerie, and Pedwyn Dale was one of the few who could find them. While there exist various troops of the little people, from the Elves to the Sprites, Goblins, Trows,

Pillywiggins, or even the Phooka; Pedwyn Dale was solitary. Somewhere in ages past human blood mingled with the Fae and only those with the blood of both worlds could venture long enough into the Mists to find the elusive elderberry. Pedwyn Dale felt important.

A good day's haul usually consisted of three to four clumps of berries, but today was beginning to appear below average. Pedwyn Dale had yet to locate a single bush when after several hours of looking; he finally gave up and took a nap. Dreams in the Faerie Mists are unexplainable things so there is no knowing of what caused Pedwyn Dale to come awake with such a start. However, he did seem very upset.

"Goodness me, the King will be fit, Mr. Dale," he stammered.

"Goodness me," he repeated.

After several more unsuccessful hours of searching, Pedwyn Dale was becoming flustered. He began to mutter to himself of several things the King would most likely say in his displeasure. Sweat began to form on Pedwyn Dale's face, and he ran his gnarled little hand over his beard repeating his predictions of the King's scolding.

"I must say I am disappointed, Pedwyn Dale," he imitated in his best impression of the King of Hollow Hill.

"I must say I expected more from you, Pedwyn Dale. However will I be able to have my party now? I have not the berries to mull enough wine to get a Dink drunk," he continued, knowing how serious that was being as how Dinks do not drink, nor do they have a need to be drunk since life for them is a never-ending series of songs and happy places.

Pedwyn Dale was determined not to have to hear those imitations of his come to light, so he continued looking. One has to be very careful in the Mist, for there are several holes leading to the human world and untold dangers within. Pedwyn Dale, in his haste not to upset the King, left his customary caution behind.

So it was, that Pedwyn Dale found himself in the middle of a rain storm in a small patch of wood. He barely caught a glimpse of a large loud speeding blue object before he realized his mistake and dove back through the closing Mist-hole as it shrank around his foot.

3

"Mommmm! Dadddd! Looook! Look over there did you see him? Did you?" Tad Tucker was screaming. "Dadd! turn around dad please, turn around!" he hollered. Tads' father barely avoided running off the road during his son's outburst. Erin jolted from her sleep with a startled yelp.

"Young man you will stop yelling this second," his mother scolded.

"But MOM..., Tad started, I just saw...."

"I said this second, Thaddeus!" his mother said. He hated when she called him that.

"What did he see, mom? Erin asked.

"Nothing dear, your brother is just upset about the game, now lie back down," his mother said, totally missing the point. Sure, he was upset about the game, but that had nothing to do with his outburst, the little man did. He pleaded once more.

"Dad, please turn around. I swear I just saw...,"

"Enough!" his mother yelled, "not another word, you are scaring your sister."

"Maybe he did see something," his dad said, still trying to remain calm with all the clamor going on around him. "What was it, son?" he asked.

"Stop it, Ronald," his mother said bitterly, "Stop trying to undermine me."

"I am not trying to undermine you, Helen. I just...." His father's voice trailed off as Tad shut out his parents' argument. He could not believe they were turning this into another fight. He also could not believe what he had seen.

"What was it, Tad?" Erin asked, sounding interested, not scared. He decided to try and tell her. Heck, he had to tell someone.

"Do you promise not to laugh?" Tad asked his sister. "Do you promise to believe me?"

"I promise," she replied giggling, "now what was it?"

He told her about the little man, about his shabby white shirt and the tattered dirty clothing he wore, his droopy red hat, his bucket, every detail he could remember. He even mentioned the surprised look on the fellow's face.

"His eyes were THIS big," he said, indicating how big with his fingers. Erin listened intently through the whole description while their parents continued their arguing. After her brother finished, she stared up at him for a few seconds with Barbie lying forgotten in her lap. She was six years old and intelligent beyond her age, so it surprised Tad little to hear her scoff at his story.

"Really," she stated sardonically, and closed her eyes in an attempt to fall back to the rain-induced sleep she was enjoying before her brother's eruption.

"Fine, don't believe me," Tad said loud enough for the whole car to hear him. No one seemed to care enough to comment, and the remainder of the ride home was spent in silence. Tad knew who would listen to his story; his best friend in the whole world, Luke Monroe.

Luke Monroe was, by every fourth-grade definition, a geek. His only true love was math. Math for gosh sakes! Tad had never understood why his friend so preoccupied his time with the science, but he liked Luke, nonetheless. Few other people did. Tad himself had made few friends in his school, and one too many enemies in Chuck Bain - which reminded him of Monday; Luke had even less. Still, Luke would believe his friend.

Tad decided to call Luke before he even changed out of his game clothes. Luke Monroe came over later that night and the two boys met in Tad's well-constructed tree house. His dad built the tree house years ago and it was still the envy of every boy in town, even Chuck Bain, though he would never admit it.

"What's up, Tad?" Luke asked, "Why did you sound so urgent on the phone? My mom says I can only stay a little while. I have to study for our math test."

"Our math test isn't for another week, Luke!" said Tad.

23

"You know me, Thaddeus," Luke said, giggling at using his friend's real name. Tad gave him a playful hit on the arm.

"Stop that," Tad said, "now listen, we have been friends for how long now?" he asked.

"Since first grade," his friend replied.

"And who saved your life from Chuck Bain last year when you spilt your chocolate milk on his homework?" Tad continued.

"You saved me by promising him I would do his homework for the rest of the year," Luke said, "He probably would have been held back if not for me."

"Never mind that," Tad said, "he was going to kill you."

"OK, OK, what is your point?" Luke wondered.

"If I were to tell you I saw something," Tad explained, "and this something was very hard to believe, but I swore to you by our friendship that I had seen it, would you believe me?" Tad asked, hoping for the right answer.

"What did you see? Luke asked.

"Swear first to believe me," Tad demanded.

"OK, I swear, now what are you talking about?" Luke said impatiently.

Tad gazed around the tree house; he leaned out the doorway and looked down the ladder making sure they were alone. Tad leaned in close to his friend. Luke was starting to sense the seriousness of the situation and his curiosity was near bursting. Tad checked down the ladder again.

"Will you please tell me!" Luke shouted, grabbing Tad and shaking him.

"I saw an Elf, Luke! I swear! I saw an Elf," he whispered hoarsely, still afraid someone might be nearby. An Elf is what he convinced himself it was, finding no other explanation. While in truth, Pedwyn Dale was no Elf, but Tad had no way of knowing this yet.

Tad waited for some similar response like the one received from Erin, but Luke just stared at him.

"Where?" Luke asked simply.

"You believe me then?" Tad said relieved, "I knew you would, Luke. I knew you would." I saw him today after my soccer game while we were driving home near Wheeler's Pond."

"Did you win?" Luke asked.

"No!" Tad yelled, "Who cares about the stupid game, did you hear me or not?"

"When you say Elf, how do you mean," Luke said, "Do you mean like a Santa Elf?"

"I don't know," Tad yelled, "What kind of elves are there? Heck, I don't know."

"What did he look like? Was it a "he," his friend said, trying hard to sound like he did indeed believe.

Tad began to relate the details of his sighting to his friend, just as he did with his sister. He told Luke everything about the game, about the rain, his parents' fight, everything, and especially about the little man. When he was finished Luke was silent for a few seconds before he finally spoke.

"Tad," he said, "you've gotta know how hard this is to swallow."

"Sure," Tad said in agreement, "OK, promise me this. Tomorrow, after school, we ride our bikes out there and have a look around. What about that?"

"I don't know, Tad," his friend said sheepishly, "Wheeler's Pond is an awful long way off, and I have to study tomorrow you know."

"Will you please forget about studying for once in your life, Luke?" Tad yelled, "This is our chance to be famous, our chance to show the whole school what's what. If we can catch this thing then we would be heroes, who knows what, maybe even be on TV. Please Luke, just this once, for me. Please."

"Alright, but this better be good," Luke said, "And I have to get home before my folks."

"Done," Tad said with a smile, "Thanks buddy, I knew I could count on you, see you tomorrow alright?"

"Yeah OK, see you tomorrow, Tad," Luke said as he climbed down the tree house ladder, retrieved his bicycle, and slowly pedaled beneath the warm buzzing streetlights toward home.

Tad sped inside and climbed the stairs immediately to his room. He could hear his parents through their door and wondered if their fighting would ever end. No matter, he had other things to think of, like tomorrow's journey.

Tad Tucker lay in his bed and thought about his day. It had started out horrible with the soccer loss, but that seemed so far away now. Sure, Chuck Bain would tease him tomorrow, and he would feel embarrassed when he saw Patty Greene, but no matter. Tomorrow he was going to find this Elf, and no one was going to look down on Tad Tucker again. He would show them. He slowly drifted off to sleep wondering if Patty liked Elves and thinking that Monday was not going to be that bad after all.

4

Tad awoke earlier than usual the next morning. He grabbed the lunch his mother had packed for him from its usual spot and bolted out the door. Luke met Tad as always behind the school cafeteria; this being as far away from where Chuck Bain hung out in the mornings. They locked up their bikes and walked silently towards the classroom. An uneasy tension always accompanied them until they were safely inside the door. Those of you with bully experience can relate. When they finally made it inside, Tad could no longer hold his excitement.

"Well," he said, "are you ready to go?"

"Oh man," Luke said slowly, "I was hoping that you weren't serious."

"Not serious!?" Tad yelled, "I didn't sleep at all last night, and it's all I can do to make it until school lets out."

"Well alright," Luke resigned, "let's go find your Elf. But remember Tad, I have to be home before my parents are."

"Did you bring the things I asked for?" Tad wondered.

"One butterfly net and one fully loaded camera." Luke said, proud to admit his household was the only one in town that one could ask for, and receive, a butterfly net.

"Great job, pal," said Tad.

29

Tad's day wore slowly on from that point. His teacher talked, but nothing got through to him. His mind was on one thing, his Elf. He wandered the halls between classes in a daze. What would his classmates think when he showed them the little man? He could see himself with Patty as the Elf danced for them and made her smile. Oh man, he thought, he was going to be the most popular fourth grader ever.

"Tadpole Tucker!!!!" the scream came from behind him. "Hey Tadpole, where ya going?" It was Chuck Bain. Tad winced, and slowly turned around.

"Hi Chuck," Tad said, "I'm on my way to..."

"Shut up, punk!" Bain yelled, "Who asked you a question?"

"You did Chu..."

"I said shut up, Tadpole," Bain snorted. He was escorted by the usual rabble that sucked up to him and he was about to impress them all by humiliating Tad.

"Nice game yesterday..." Chuck said. Tad waited.

"...for a GIRL!!!" Bain finished. Tad bit his lip as Bain's cronies crawled with laughter and pointed fingers at him condescendingly.

Tad reddened as Bain continued to tell the now larger crowd about his game winner. Tad really became red when he noticed Patty among the gathering. "Just wait," he found himself saying aloud.

"Just wait for what?" Bain said, "For you to grow boobs like all the other girls?"

This produced snickers from the crowd and Tad was mortified as he noticed even Patty Greene shyly giggling. He told himself that he would show them all tomorrow and before he realized it, he had spoken aloud again. Chuck Bain glared at him for a second as if contemplating socking him in the nose. Tad closed his eyes.

Just then a teacher called for the kids to get to class and stop gathering in the halls. This sent most everyone scurrying, except Chuck Bain.

"I'm really looking forward to your little surprise tomorrow, Tucker" he said, pounding his fist into his hand. Tad swallowed and wished he had kept his mouth shut.

"What happens tomorrow?" a voice said from behind.

Tad wheeled to find Patty standing behind him. She was beautiful and her innocent hazel-hued eyes hit Tad harder than Chuck Bain's fists ever could. He hesitated for a second, not quite sure what to say as she continued to look at him.

"Can you keep a secret?" he asked.

5

The King of Hollow Hills' party had been a complete failure. The Shee-Queen visited from the Farland, and the King had so wanted to impress her with the jolliest revelry ever. What *could* go wrong, *did* go wrong, and now all the Faerie Folk were summoned to the Shale for a scolding. The Shale was what passed for prison in the land of the Fae. No singing, nor dancing, was permitted inside Shale walls. This restriction on merriment is mostly unbearable to endure for the little ones who are condemned there. A Faery must be able to sing or dance at some point, so most sentences are light. However, the King was in a foul mood, and all gathered were fearful of spending the night inside the Shale, all except Pedwyn Dale.

Pedwyn Dale stood in the back of the main gathering hall, looking over the crowd of fellow Faeries with mild regard. He wondered which of them caused the King's anger, who spoiled the party, and more importantly for his own curiosity, how they were caught doing it. His suspicions whispered in his thoughts as the notable troublemakers of Hollow Hill were all in attendance, and if Pedwyn Dale were forced to guess, certain names would immediately spring to mind. There were some fellow folks in his vicinity he found himself avoiding eye contact with due to not wanting to see the guilt on their faces. He kept his head down low, dawdling with his fraying beard and flicking at the floor with his big toe. Pedwyn Dale feared no Shale walls this night; his required task for the party having been ultimately accomplished. Although the Mists proved unpredictable and hazardous, Pedwyn Dale had gathered a bounty of elderberries and the King seemed more than pleased. So what was all the fuss? Exhausted from a day spent searching, Pedwyn had not bothered to go to the party - and actually had fallen asleep and forgotten - but he was beginning to understand events did not go as the King had hoped. He was wiggling his toes on the cold stone floor trying to pull the hole of his sock over them when the door beside him opened and the Judge entered the hall.

The Judge of the Shale was a rather tall Grey Elf, who for a Faery, wore untraditional black. Bent and aged, his skin resembled tree bark and his movements seemed deliberate and purposeful as he strode silently through the parting gathering to his seat. His name was unknown to Pedwyn Dale, but the Judge knew everyone's name in Hollow Hill. He garnered a sort of respect from the little people mostly due to his ability to get them in trouble. Most all Faeries pulled some sort of overboard prank sooner or later, and the Judge always reprimanded them for it. He sat rigid and straight, his eyes scanning the room slowly, uncomfortably for those meeting their gaze. A sense of uneasiness spread like a blanket across the hall as the Judge continued to scan the crowd accusingly. All became quite when he rose and spoke:

"The King is mad.

The King is sad.

He has taken all your bad.

If you have not sneaked out by now,

you might wish you had."

With his opening lines having worried the crowd into silence, he began to call the names of the accused. It started with the lesser offenders: some Knockers who wore mismatched knickers; a Kobold who violently burped during the Queen's entry; Mik-of-the-Lob who egotistically kept annoying everyone to look at his self-portrait drawing when in fact it was not very well done; and finally to Blee the Brownie, who had pooted during the Silent Seconds and caused everyone, including the Queen, to giggle uncontrollably. The King of Hollow Hill had not giggled, and poor dyspeptic Blee paid the price. More light sentences followed with the procedure taking the better part of the day and Pedwyn Dale was becoming restless, not to mention his toes were freezing on the cold floor.

The Judge continued to hand down time in the Shale, and the Fae Folk continued to murmur when sentences of several hours were given. Finally, the Judge came to the presumed serious agitators. Pedwyn Dale stood on his half-exposed tip-toes to get a better view. As he watched and listened, the picture of the King's spoiled party became clearer. First, there was BeBoo Pevin.

BeBoo was a Pixie and the gardener of the King. He fancied himself somewhat of a Medium and was always trying to cast a spell or two which usually went the opposite way from his intention. He was about nine inches tall and a pale minty-green color, as were most Pixie. He wore a deerskin cap with his ears poked through and his eyes barely peeped from beneath the brim. His nose and chin jutted from his small face, and while he wore tattered little brown shoes, he rarely bothered with clothes. BeBoo grinned nervously at the Judge. He swayed back and forth from foot to foot and made all present slightly more anxious. Apparently, BeBoo had been assigned by the King to plant a row of cowslips around the castle walls before the party. The Shee-Queen was fond of the pretty yellow flower and the King wanted her to feel at home. BeBoo, in his laziness, had waited until the last day to plant them. Realizing his mistake, he cast a Growth spell on the seeds to rush them up to full height. Needless to say, the Pixie's spell went awry causing the cowslips to grow so wildly they covered the entire entryway forcing the guests to crawl into the party. The King was not happy. Again, the Judge spoke:

"Cowslip that you planted,

flowers you enchanted,

made the King displeased,

from on his hands and knees,

Shale-time...two weeks"

The gathered Fae gasped in horror. Two weeks! Pedwyn Dale dropped his mouth open. He felt sorry for BeBoo Pevin. BeBoo was escorted out of the room, his hopeful grin fading. He was joined by Hetchy the Bogie who had managed to get inside the party early and eat every bit of the food, even going so far as to bite a few plates and cups.

Following behind the Pixie and the Bogie was the Spriggan, Wippa. Spriggans are the most notorious pranksters in Faerie, and Wippa was certainly no exception. These thorny spindly creatures find humor in things which would cause most other law-abiding citizens to blanch in fear. Ages ago, the Spriggans delighted in abducting human babies from their birthing cribs and replacing them with Spriggan brats. To the Spriggans this caused knee-slapping hilarity and it was impossible to explain to them the horrible effects and dismay it caused to the human parents. Eventually, the powers that be in the Faerie community enforced enough restrictions on this practice to end it, but the Spriggans quickly adapted to avenues of physical grief, or crop blighting, more so than mental anguish. Only the Shee-Queen was spared from a prickle-thorn in the seat of her chair. The King was not so fortunate. Pedwyn watched as the Bogie and the Spriggan were escorted from the chamber. He did not feel sorrow for Hetchy or Wippa as they were Shale regulars and seldom sang or danced anyway. However, he and everyone present were shocked to hear the name of the next defendant. Fee the Dink stood about three inches tall. Dinks were bright colored fairies and Fee shone a clear baby blue. Her tiny head ended in a curly-cue sprout and her fingers and toes were well out of proportion to her small teardrop shaped body. Diminutive black dot eyes sat on her round face over her always smiling mouth. What could Fee the Dink have done wrong? Pedwyn wondered.

After the Judge spoke, Pedwyn Dale did not know whether to laugh or shout out in cheer for the little Dink. It appears that while the King was scolding the Goblin guards on the importance of not letting any undesirables inside - like Bogies or Spriggans - Fee the Dink flew up and kissed him on the cheek. This caused the King to giggle out loud and the Goblins to not take his statement so seriously. Hence, everyone sat on prickle-thorn seats at a table with no food. Pedwyn did not think it fair the Dink should be blamed for all this, and actually found it quite amusing, but the King felt differently. Fee cooed a long sad whistle as she was led to the murky back hallways of the Shale. Pedwyn Dale was once again feeling the coldness of the stone floor when the Judge spoke again:

"Now listen friends and listen keen,

Like the fish are wont in the bubble stream,

One has done the never deed,

Like Unicorn, like Mermaid creed,

One has turned the King to green,

One among you has been seen!!!"

Pedwyn Dale nearly chocked on his beard - which he as usual had in his mouth. Seen! Being seen - by humans - was the worst thing a Faerie denizen could do. It was the ultimate mistake and almost always led to banishment or worse. Pedwyn Dale began to feel very sorry for whoever the Judge was referring to as he again tried to get his toe back into his sock hole. Who was it he wondered? How did it happen?

The Faerie Folk were all talking at once in a mix of hushed voices. All knew the price for being seen. The Wee Folk could not take chances like letting the humans know of their existence. The Unicorns and the Mermaids had done it long ago and look what it brought them. The Judge came down off his seat and began to walk around the room as if looking for the guilty one. Pedwyn Dale looked around at the nervous faces near him as the Judge meandered purposefully through the crowd. Most all were holding their breath as the Judge finally stopped. Pedwyn looked around to see who the Judge was looking at and felt a lump in his throat when he realized it was him.

"Pedwyn Dale," the Judge asked, "where is your shoe?"

<u>6</u>

"Looook!!!" Tad Tucker was screaming.

"Oh my God, Luke, look!" he continued, still not believing what he was seeing. In his hand Tad Tucker held a shoe. The shoe was roughly two inches long and dull black. A tiny tarnished brass buckle adorned the vamp, and a rather unpleasant stale, acrid odor emanated from the shoe's lining.

Luke wrinkled his nose at the smell as he peered closer at the little shoe.

"Phew," he said, "I think your Elf needs to wash his feet."

"You believe me now then?" Tad asked hopefully.

"Well, I suppose you did see something" his friend replied. "Maybe it was a doll?" Luke continued, hoping Tad would agree. The reality that his friend might really have seen an Elf was beginning to create some strange thoughts for Luke Monroe. It could not be true, could it?

"Doll feet don't stink, Luke," Tad said, causing Luke's confusing thoughts to linger.

"I suppose not," Luke said, allowing himself to sink even further into his own belief. "What are you going to do with it, Tad?" he asked.

"We're going to show it to everyone!" Tad said with a gloating smile.

"I don't think that's a very good idea just yet," Luke added, "It was all I could do to keep you from blabbering it to Patty Greene in the hall today. I don't think we should tell anyone until we have more proof."

"More proof?" Tad yelled, "Luke look at this shoe, what more proof do we need?"

"Well, for starters we could have an Elf to wear that shoe, Tad" Luke said, hoping to convince his friend. Tad looked down at his prize. Luke believed him now at least and maybe his friend was right, maybe he should wait. Still, it was going to be hard to keep this a secret.

"Luke!" Tad said excitedly, "Can you stay in the tree house with me this weekend?"

Luke began to suspect Tad's reasoning. "Sure, I guess, but what about the test...?"

"LUKE!" Tad yelled.

"Alright, alright, I'll try, but not if I don't get home before my parents!" Luke said.

"OK, let's go, but swear first not to tell anyone until the time is right," Tad said.

"I most assuredly swear," Luke said.

"Swear on our heroes," Tad said, knowing the implications of betraying faith in any of the sports stars, comic book characters, or movie idols the boys traded stories and drew pictures about.

"I swear on our heroes," Luke Monroe finished, and the two boys left Wheeler's Pond with dreams of popularity and one very malodorous Elf shoe.

7

The Goblin stood roughly two feet tall while smelling of marsh plants and old mud. His name was JubJub, and he had been a guard at the Shale for many years. JubJub wore oily iron wrappings around decaying rags and carried with him a thick gnarled limb with a pointed end to appear as if he were threatening. His drool-covered fangs often scraped together in an annoying way and when he was trying to frighten some poor soul, he would tighten his brow to appear even uglier. This technique was having little effect on his current target; BeBoo Pevin.

"Might it trouble you JubJub to take your lovely face somewhere else for a while?" BeBoo asked, knowing how much Goblins hated to be complimented. "Your beauty is causing me to swoon," he said with a smirk. JubJub snorted and continued to stare down at the imprisoned Faeries.

"Me not no pretty!" the Goblin stammered.

"Oh, but you are so, Jubby" BeBoo said. The other Faeries began to take notice of this encounter and Fee cooed amusingly.

"No me no!" JubJub yelled.

"Yes, you yes," BeBoo retorted.

Fee flew into the air whistling several high pitched giggle noises. Hetchy the Bogie seemed not to care, while prying up small pieces of the floor and devouring them. "Blortch," he managed to turn his head and utter. Wippa the Spriggan sat and stared at the dimwitted Goblin guard, his gaze a hard-to-read mixture of amusement and utter contempt. Pedwyn Dale continued to sit in the corner, his head between his knees in disbelief over his current surroundings.

"Me make Pixie-pie out of you Pevin," JubJub threatened, as BeBoo continued to shower him with mock affection.

"If you don't believe me then just go look for yourself," BeBoo said, "There's a mirror down the hall," he lied. JubJub spat and slowly began to walk in that direction.

"Me not no going to look," he also lied, "Me got other things to do." With that, the Goblin walked haltingly down the hall, and the air around the cell was for the time being more breathable.

"Ta-Ta," BeBoo said as JubJub walked away. He then turned to his fellows with a triumphant smile. "You're welcome," he bowed. Wippa merely stuck out his tongue and muttered something unintelligible - and unmentionable - to show his opinion of the whole event, while Hetchy continued to nibble away the floor noisily, and Pedwyn continued to pout.

"Critics," BeBoo frowned, "What about you Fee? Did you like the way I handled the Goblin?"

Fee held her breath for a few seconds, her small head swelling up to twice its normal size before she let out a long, shrill beep.

"Thank you," BeBoo said with a smile.

Eventually the Pixie gave up trying to get any acclaim from his other cellmates and went back to sulking. JubJub and some of the other Goblin guards returned and beat upon the cell door scolding Fee to stop with her whistles. They considered her soundings too close to singing.

Pedwyn continued to mope. He hung his head down between his legs and wished he were anywhere but here. How had he been seen? He was only there for a second. What was the King going to do with him? He was probably going to banish him from Faerie. Pedwyn Dale was not having a good day.

Suddenly a sound came from down the hallway. A door had opened. Pedwyn looked up to see what his fate was going to be and saw BeBoo down on his knees. Fee the Dink stood by his side staring out into the hallway, and even Wippa and Hetchy had stopped their actions to gaze through the cell bars. It was then that Pedwyn noticed the whole of the room was filled with a pale-yellow glow. He turned in the direction his friends were looking and found himself meeting eyes with the Shee-Queen.

8

The Shee-Queen stood in the hallway looking into the cell at Pedwyn Dale and his companions. She was tall, radiant, and glowing with golden illumination which lighted the hallway and cell. JubJub was standing away from her, shielding his narrow eyes from her beautiful light. Her gown was of a deep forest green flowing to the floor, giving no hint towards the rumor she did not touch the ground when she walked. Several Pillywiggins flitted on honeybees about her, singing songs in strange tongues older than the first spring, adding to the overall mystique of the Queen. Her amber-colored skin shown with the same radiance she emitted as she peered down upon the inhabitants of the cell. Her sculpted face with its perfect angles showed her vast intelligence as she seemed to be studying the situation at hand. Large almond-shaped eyes of various colors stared into Pedwyn, and he felt as if he were going to explode with nervousness. Even BeBoo Pevin was somehow for the moment speechless.

"I have come from the Farlands," the Shee-Queen spoke, "as a guest of your King." Her voice seemed to ring as if she were speaking into the wind. Pedwyn thought that it reminded him of the Seas of Faerie. When the ocean breeze blew over the waves, it sometimes sounded like words.

"I was to be a guest of his at a party," she added. This caused all assembled to have an enormous surge of guilt over the fact they had in some way contributed to the party going off-center. Fee the Dink cooed long and sad and hung her little head down. Wippa turned away to avoid the Shee-Queen's gaze. Whatever amount of guilt a Spriggan can feel, he felt. Hetchy would have said something for himself if he could. It should be noted here that Bogies are nefarious eaters. They, in fact, are so busy eating from the very moment of their birth that they rarely bother with learning how to talk. Words coming out of their mouths tend to get in the way of whatever is going in at the time. So the Bogie made no sound. BeBoo and Pedwyn were not burdened with this ailment and they both shouted out simultaneously.

"Please forgive us, your Majesty, we never meant to disturb your party," they shouted. Pedwyn, in his haste, realized he had actually not disturbed the party but had done something far worse. Maybe, he thought, if he acted like he was guilty of the party mess, she would forget his being seen.

"Pedwyn Dale, you were seen," the Queen accused him softly. Pedwyn's hopes came crashing down, and he with them, to the hard, cold, stone floor.

"Yes," he spoke, "It appears that I was." "Where will I be banished, your Highness?" he asked, "Will it be Gail? or Adder? or worse, Kel?" he said, hoping for any of those three since none was as bad as the Nil Fields, which were where banishments were normally sent.

"Are you so quick to leave your surroundings, friend Dale?" the Shee-Queen asked, "so quick to give up your profession, your friends, your home?" She gazed down on Pedwyn as she asked this and kept herself from grinning over his preoccupation with trying to get his toe into his sock hole.

Pedwyn Dale looked up towards the Queen. His answer reflected in his face. He loved his job, his friends, and the fields of his home. He would do anything to be able to make amends for his fault. Tears welled up in his eyes, and the Queen effortlessly stepped through the bars to touch his forehead.

"My little one," she said, "would that I should be the ruler of these lands with the joke-makers and the flower-lovers. You are indeed the jewels of Faerie, while my Kingdom bears the heavy weight of serious matters. Long at night does my mind wander and miss the days of bare feet running through the hills and singing with the little ones of the stream. The years run like rain off the roofs of our houses, Pedwyn Dale, and I would take none of them from you. Nor would I condemn you or your companions a minute more of life behind these cruel walls. But you must answer for your deed, friend Dale. You must right what you have done wrong lest you bring about trouble for your neighbors."

"What can I do, your Grace?" Pedwyn pleaded, a hope welling up inside him that he might escape his grim predicted future.

"You must away to the place of sight," she said, "and you must bring to the mind of the beholder a way to forget."

"I do not understand, Fair One, where am I to go? What am I to bring?" he asked.

"The World, my friend, you must go to the World and seek the one who has seen you. You must cause him to forget that this sighting ever was," the Shee-Queen spoke. With that she handed Pedwyn Dale a small bale of wrappings.

"What is this, your Majesty? Pedwyn asked.

"Inside you will find the means to complete your task," the Shee-Queen replied.

Pedwyn Dale took one of the small packages and slowly began to unwrap it, pulling a tightly bound string and releasing the silken leafy folds of the outer wrapper. Inside a blueish-yellow rectangular slab was exposed.

"Mooncheese!" BeBoo Pevin excitedly proclaimed as he leaned in for a closer look.

"Yes, little one, the slices of the moon will cause those who eat them to forget all that they no longer need know," she answered. Pedwyn pulled one of the slices out of its leafy wrapping.

"It looks just like real cheese," he said.

"You must feed this to the one who has seen you, friend Dale," the Shee-Queen spoke, "I will deliver you to the place of sighting and you must from there journey to the home of the Tucker."

"The Tucker?" he asked, "Who is the Tucker?"

"The name of he who has seen you, little one, and he must be made to eat the Mooncheese," she said. "Too long has it been since the races of Men and Faerie have sung the same songs, and the humans are not ready to accept our existence." "They would be curious to the point of danger, friend Dale, and we must NOT allow them to harm all that we have built here." Turning towards the others, her gaze seemed more serious. "My children, you must away with Mr. Dale to the World. The crimes your King has accused you of will be forgiven upon your return." The Faeries seemed pleased with this punishment. Wippa began to immediately plot the many pranks he could pull on the humans, while Hetchy wondered what they had to eat on the World. BeBoo seemed most eager to go and began to limber up his fingers with the notion he would no doubt use them many times for spellcasting during the trip. The Shee-Queen looked at him accusingly as she warned the group to be careful.

"You should not tarry friend Dale," she said, "go at once to the home of the Tucker and complete your task. I am giving each of you a piece of the Mooncheese in case any of you are seen during your venture, although I should trust that you will represent your species well by staying hidden, which is and always should be our kind's best asset."

With that the Shee-Queen vanished slowly in front of the surprised Faeries. Wisps of smoke and the scent of flowers filled the cell during her departure. The door was standing open and JubJub was nowhere to be seen. Pedwyn Dale and his companions began to slowly exit their place of punishment, and eventually, and much quicker, they left the corridors and the damp rooms of the Shale behind.

"What do we do now?" Pedwyn asked.

"We go home and pack, that's what," BeBoo replied excitedly, "I'm going to bring my Star-Hat, my Glee-Wand, my See-Scope..." Pedwyn cut BeBoo off before he could list his entire inventory.

"I do not think that is a good idea, Pixie," he said, "in fact I do not think that is a very wise idea at all, Glee-Wands and See-Scopes indeed. "

"Why not?" BeBoo demanded, "I have wanted to see the World since I was a wee Pixen and here I am finally getting my chance, by dingit, I will bring my things!" he added with authority, causing Pedwyn to relent.

"My goodness," Pedwyn said, "goodness me indeed, don't get rolled up about it. I am just saying that the Shee-Queen told us to be careful, and I seem to remember her giving you a very special look at the same time as she said it, I do."

"Really?" BeBoo asked, sounding serious, "I don't seem to recall that at all."

"Oh never mind!" Pedwyn said, storming away nervously muttering to himself, as BeBoo smiled proudly and scampered to his village to pack. With that the reluctant companions went their separate ways, agreeing to meet that night after they had gathered their things and said good-byes to their families - and eaten a few times in Hetchy's case. Pedwyn returned to his house where his day had started, silently sinking down into this chair. He thought to himself how it must have been a week ago when he had picked the elderberries but in reality, he realized it had been a very long couple of days. Seconds later, with beard in mouth, Pedwyn Dale was asleep.

9

Tad Tucker quickly readied for school the next morning. His excitement was peaking as he raced out the door much earlier than his normal routine. His best friend, slightly less excited, met him along the way. Together, and in silence, they went about their daily routine of hiding their bikes in the back of the school yard and walked un-bullied into the building.

"Are you still serious about this?" Luke Monroe asked.

"Absolutely serious," Tad replied, "I wouldn't worry so much if I were you Luke, no one is gonna laugh, not now, I have proof!" He held up the little black shoe so his friend could see it again. The odor was still recognizable even though Tad had spent the better part of an hour cleaning the foul-smelling footwear.

"Still stinks," Luke said wrinkling his nose. "Tad, I just don't think the time is right to expose this thing yet, I mean let's find the Elf first, OK?" he pleaded.

"Luke, I know that you think everyone is going to laugh at me, but don't worry, I won't mention your name, OK?" Tad said.

"I still think it's a bad idea," said Luke.

"Just wait," Tad replied.

Tad and Luke took their seats in the front of the class and the ever present sense of being watched overtook them. Chuck Bain sat in the back with his followers. Their conversation stalled as soon as Tad and Luke entered the room, and Chuck began to glare at Tad like a hunter does to his prey. Tad swallowed. He always planned to delay his entrance into the classroom until it timed with the teacher, but in his excitement he and Luke had forgotten this tactic and were now at Bain's mercy.

"Tadpole and Puke," Chuck Bain sneered, his upper lip curling in an eerie sort of way. The rest of the classroom sensed a confrontation and fell hushed. Tad and Luke both slowly turned around.

"We are all anxiously waiting for your surprise, Tucker" Bain continued, "I hope for your sake that it's worth the wait." Bain reached into his pocket and pulled out a black weight lifting glove, slowly fitting it onto his hand. Dark rumors spread throughout Southern Shores Middle School that this same glove caused Derrick Bowden to visit Dr. Webb's dental establishment more than once. Tad felt his heart in his throat. Mrs. Littlefield walked fortuitously into the room, saving him from what seemed like instant doom. Chuck Bain shot him a look of contempt as he and Luke turned back towards the front of the class. This brush with aggression would normally have caused Tad Tucker to be wary, but his welling excitement to show up everyone overrode normal feelings of victim angst.

66

"Mrs. Littlefield," he said, "are we having Show and Tell today?"

"Yes, Mr. Tucker," she replied, "but not until the end of class time, today we are going to begin learning cursive writing."

The remainder of the class dragged slowly on for Tad Tucker, until finally Mrs. Littlefield put down her chalk and sat behind her desk. "Now," she asked, "does anyone have anything for Show and Tell?" Tad Tucker was the first to raise his hand.

Tad stood at the head of the class, and the way he began to relate his story held the attention of everyone, even Chuck Bain. He finished with a "and then we found this!" which caused Luke to sink into his chair with conscious horror assuming everyone would know who the "we" was in Tad's sentence. Tad held the little black shoe up for everyone to see and the children all crowded around him to look. Patty Greene stood on tip-toes behind everyone, and Tad held out his hand to make sure she could see it better.

Tad began to tell everyone how he planned to return to the spot where he found the shoe, being careful not to reveal the secret location, and capture the Elf to which it belonged. Tad's classmates began to stare at him in wonder, some struggling with belief, others holding back laughter. All of them seemed to be waiting for someone to say something. Chuck Bain did not let them down.

"Did that come off one of your Barbie Dolls, little girl?" he jeered. Giggles erupted around them, and Luke, who remained in his seat during the entire presentation, now sank even lower in an effort not to be noticed. He warned Tad this would happen.

"All right children," Mrs. Littlefield interrupted, "return to your seats please. That was a very interesting story, Tad. I trust you will show us any and all future discoveries that you find. I would be very interested in seeing your Elf," she added, trying to make Tad feel better. He could sense she really did not believe him, and any classmates who might have believed were swayed back by Bain's comment. That was alright he thought, he would find this Elf and show them all. Let them laugh now he thought, soon they would all know he was telling the truth.

"Interesting Tucker," Chuck Bain whispered from behind him as the other students were showing off their own items. "I was gonna pulverize you today but now I think that you are so weird I might catch something if I hit you, besides, I wouldn't want your big bad old Elf to come and get me," he laughed. Tad Tucker sat at his desk silently enduring Chuck's torment while other kids showed off their toys, old pictures of their mother and father, and countless other things nowhere near as special as an Elf shoe. A storm began to well up inside him, and he let it all come out at once, the soccer game loss, his parents' fighting, Chuck Bain's torment, Patty Greene seeing his humiliation, and no one believing his story, all caused him to snap. He turned in his seat and grabbed Chuck by his shirt and shook him.

"I did see him, I did!" Tad shouted, all the while shaking Chuck Bain violently. Chuck Bain reacted the only way he knew how, whacking Tad right between the eyes. Luke watched this all play out from his vantage point which at this time was practically sitting on the floor. The class reacted as all classes do when encountering a fight, and soon the combatants were surrounded by eager spectators. Mrs. Littlefield quickly restored order with both boys finding themselves in the Principal's office. This day was supposed to have gone wonderful for Tad Tucker, but he soon realized it was not going to be. He had to find that Elf he thought.

10

That Elf was currently standing on the banks of a large ditch desperately trying to find a way across. His companions were busying themselves with this same task, except Hetchy who was snacking on some marsh reeds.

"Wuspumpf mewl kisy," he said, as a small frog leapt safely from his maw amidst clumps of mud and clay.

Let us again remind ourselves that Pedwyn Dale is not an Elf. Elves are slender, graceful creatures with more magic in them than most of the denizens of Faerie. It is said they can walk upon the snow without leaving a footprint, hear the fall of each leaf, and dance upon the blades of grass. Pedwyn had already tripped and fallen four times since arriving on the World.

"Goodness me!" he shouted after the fourth fall, "Where are all these bumps coming from? Does anyone see a way over this ditch? he asked, "BeBoo stop that!"

Pedwyn yelled at the Pixie who was waving his Glee-Wand at the far bank of the ditch in an attempt to pull the other side towards them. He had donned his Star-Hat as well, and the golden star which hung from the glittering silver cap now drooped in his eyes.

"Don't you remember the last time you tried that trick?" Pedwyn asked, "You flooded the whole village when you damned the river up."

"But I know how to do it now, I was younger then," BeBoo defended.

"It was last year," Pedwyn rebutted.

"Younger," the Pixie stated factually.

"Goodness," Pedwyn said rolling his eyes, "well don't try it anyhow just keep looking for a way across."

The Fae troop gathered in the grove of wood just a few feet from where Tad Tucker first spotted Pedwyn Dale. The Shee-Queen's magic deposited them there, each with their leaf wrapped Mooncheese and the mission of correcting Pedwyn's blunder. Pedwyn was most anxious to get this all over with and go back home, while the others seemed to be enjoying themselves. Wippa was silent and brooding, yet a mischievous smile spread across his face as he surveyed the world of the humans for the first time. Hetchy seemed to like the local cuisine so far, and Fee the Dink never showed any signs of being in a bad mood. She whistled and hummed while buzzing the air about Pedwyn's head. BeBoo Pevin was about to explode with the excitement welling up inside the young Pixie. No one in his family had ever traveled to the World and now he was the first. He stood brimming with pride all the while thinking that he should get in trouble with the King more often if this was the result. Pedwyn was still frantically searching for a way across when he heard rustling in the nearby undergrowth. The company scattered, melting into their surroundings, keeping their promise to the Shee-Queen to stay hidden. Pedwyn peeked from behind his hiding place to see a rather large creature emerge from the brush. It walked on four legs with its rear slightly elevated and wore grayish-brown fur with blackened eyes and feet. The creature emerged into the clearing pushing a piece of what looked like an apple. It wandered down towards the water's edge and began to methodically wash its food. Pedwyn found himself creeping closer. The others followed and were soon aside him watching this stranger creature of the World devour its now clean meal. Hetchy could no longer contain himself, and much to the other's shock, stepped from cover. The animal turned quickly, holding his food up close, and regarded the Bogie with a curious stare. Hetchy came closer and was now rudely staring at the apple chunk in the animal's paws. His mouth began to drip with desire. Pedwyn rolled his eyes and stepped from his hiding place. His companions all followed his lead. The animal crouched defensively but before it could run or act, Pedwyn spoke.

"Hello friend," he said, "don't mind Hetchy; he brings you no harm, nor do we for that matter. We are not from here and really only looking for a better path."

The animal continued to stare but sat still as if sensing no immediate danger from this collection of odd individuals. He munched on his apple and surprisingly without glancing his way tossed the Bogie a small piece, which Hetchy quickly ate right off the ground along with a few pebbles. The creature began to chitter towards Pedwyn Dale, and the listener nodded along. The blood of the World flowed in his veins and the languages of its inhabitants were clear to him.

"What is it saying?" BeBoo asked, tossing his drooping Star-Hat to one side, "And by the way, what is it, Pedwyn?"

"He is asking our business and our names. He is a very polite fellow you should know," Pedwyn said, smiling and continuing to listen to the animal's series of chitters.

"Yes, but what IS it?" BeBoo implored.

"Oh, sorry, he is a Rack Oon I think, and he is asking what we are," Pedwyn said and began to make similar noises back towards the "Rack Oon".

"Well it's obvious that I am a Pixie," BeBoo proclaimed, and was stunned when Pedwyn explained that the Rack Oon did not know what a Pixie was. "Doesn't know what a Pixie is? What sort of a place is this?" BeBoo said, plopping down on his bottom and folding his arms.

Pedwyn ignored him and continued to chat with the Rack Oon as the others nervously looked around fearful of the noise the conversation was making. After a few seconds more, Pedwyn turned to his friends and said, "He swims across the water." Wippa spat. Pedwyn frowned at the Spriggan and said, "Don't worry I told him we folk were not really made for swimming and are more designed for bridges. I asked him if there were a bridge near this spot. He is going to show us now, said there were children here earlier racing leaves in the water who built a small bridge."

"He said all that?" BeBoo asked, "Children racing leaves? Humans are odd."

Pedwyn ignored him again. The Rack Oon led the small band through the marsh grass and onto the banks of the ditch. The ditch was hopelessly wide and the strong current flowing through it confirmed Pedwyn's belief that his smaller friends would not be able to make it across - nor himself for that matter since he had never bothered to learn how to swim. The Faeries scrambled over fallen branches and crawled through tangled growths of grass and weeds to get to the point where the Rack Oon waited for them. Hetchy was thankful for the tasty berries and flowers the Rack Oon found for him along the way. He smiled and looked up, his mouth full of dirt and little purple plants.

"Frrrend," he mumbled.

The Rack Oon kept going and the rest followed him for a few more minutes before he stopped short, looking around nervously in fear.

"Something is coming," Pedwyn translated.

"From where?" BeBoo whispered, immediately pulling out his Glee-Wand from wherever it was he kept it hidden and since he did not wear clothes, no one ever asked.

"Sssshhh get down," Pedwyn said quietly, as the Faeries melted into the grass along with their animal companion. One by one, they peered out to see what it was they were hiding from. Just then, they saw two human children come speeding up on some kind of two-wheeled contraptions, stopping on the far side of the ditch edge. The Faeries shrank down low into the vegetation. Pedwyn began to worry they would be seen but the boys kept going a little farther down the ditch side, he relaxed and told the other to keep quiet. BeBoo pointed out he was the only one making any noise to begin with. Pedwyn was about to tell him to stop arguing when the children suddenly appeared almost right on top of him. He ducked quickly.

"Are you sure this is the spot, Tad?" Luke Monroe asked his friend.

"Yes, I'm sure Luke, it was over there a bit, but we already searched there so I thought maybe we should check around here some first," Tad replied, his black eye dominating his face.

"He looks like the Rack Oon," BeBoo jokingly whispered to all who could hear.

"Goodness me, hush!" Pedwyn hoarsely whispered back. He and the Pixie continued to watch the children.

"Well I hope you know that I can't stay out here long, Tad. I'm already taking a big risk coming out here after school to begin with. I wouldn't have if Chuck hadn't chased us in this direction anyway," Luke said.

"Yeah, that was convenient huh?" Tad said absentmindedly, while looking on the ground for any sign of an Elf. His mind had been on nothing else since coming out of the Principal's office. Not his black eye, not the note he was told to get his parents to sign, not Chuck Bain, or the other children, just the Elf. The boys continued to comb the area neither very sure of what they were looking for, but at least one of them desperate to find anything. The Faeries continued to watch them from their places of concealment and even Hetchy was keeping quiet, still chewing, but chewing quietly. Wippa was bored out of his Spriggan brain and could see no reason why they should be hiding. He had scooted up to Pedwyn and suggested several times they should just jump out and scare the children half to death, or better yet push them into the water while they were looking on the ditch edge. He was anxious and grinned wickedly with these suggestions, but Pedwyn vetoed them all and told him to keep quiet. Wippa hissed and crawled back to where he had been hiding. Brooding to himself and so far, unimpressed with his time on the World. The children were peering into the nearby woods when the Rack Oon emerged out of hiding and joined the Faeries. He began to chitter again excitedly, causing Pedwyn to stand on his exposed tip toes looking out over the tall grass and weeds.

"Well, what is it?" BeBoo asked.

"He says they had to have come across the bridge, we will wait for them to leave and seek it out," Pedwyn said excitedly.

The children started to double back, and the Faeries all secreted away into their surroundings. The unknowing boys walked right past them. One with his head hung low and sulking, the other with a vacant stare. The Rack Oon gave the signal once the human children were far enough away, and the troop crept softly behind him, following the boys to the bridge. Once the small humans had crossed and gone away it would be easy enough for them to follow across the bridge.

"Sorry, Tad," Luke said, "look we can come back tomorrow if you want."

"No Luke, it's no use," Tad said dejectedly. "You were right all along, I made a fool of myself today and now I'm in trouble with my parents when they find out I got into a fight, but man I just know I saw something." As he said this, he and Luke were crossing the makeshift bridge and he was looking back at the spot where he thought he had seen this Elf. He reached into his pocket and pulled out the little black shoe, eyeing the other side.

"Tad, don't," Luke said.

"Forget it," Tad said, as he launched the shoe into the brush on the other side of the ditch. The shoe flew through the air and landed inches from where its' owner was crouched hidden. Pedwyn looked at it in disbelief, suddenly realizing why he kept tripping all the time. Realization struck him, and he looked up at the boy who had thrown his footwear.

"The Tucker," he whispered to himself, "We have to get across." He told the other quietly. "Hurry, we have to follow him to give him the Mooncheese." The Faeries and the Rack Oon moved quickly towards the bridge while keeping out of sight the whole time. Pedwyn was beginning to get excited thinking that in a short time he would be back in his little house safe and warm. Just then he heard a loud splash.

"I'm never coming back here again," Tad Tucker said, as he heaved the bridge boards into the ditch. Pedwyn watched in horror as his means across was sunken beneath the rain swelled ditch water. Fee the Dink let go a loud and long "faweeeeeeeeeeeeee." This ended with a sad little "fweep," as she hung her small blue head down into her long-fingered hands.

"What was that?" Tad asked, glancing back across the water.

"Tad," Luke said softly, knowing his friend was upset, "can we just go home?" With that, the boys left Wheeler's Pond, never seeing six small figures emerge from the scrub, looking sadly at the remains of the bridge.

11

The next morning Tad ate breakfast with his family in silence. Not speaking was now normal interaction between his mother and father, but his sister's silence was unusual. Tad reluctantly realized Erin was old enough to sense something was wrong with her mom and dad, and this unhappy discovery was slowly overwhelming her childlike innocence. Erin's new sullen demeanor became one more stressor to bear. He decided he would try to talk with her later, but he was more concerned at the moment with his own fate. Attending school today was going to be difficult. Chuck Bain would be waiting, his followers jeering at his side. The rest of the kids would be expecting a repeat round of yesterday's fight, and Tad's ever yellowing black eye was an obvious sign who had won the first round. His father half-heartedly asked about the shiner, and due to welling anger over an argument with his wife, accepted his son's feigning response of a bicycle wreck. Though he knew the school had sent home a note about the incident, Tad concocted a story for now pushing off the expected punishment. Tad grabbed the brown paper bag lunch his mom always left on the counter, said his goodbyes to everyone, and was out the door.

Today Tad Tucker decided to be bold. He was going to ride his bike on a new path to school, cutting through old Mr. Jones' yard - which old Mr. Jones hated - and emerging onto Curling Street. It was no mere coincidence one Patricia Greene lived and walked to school down Curling Street at just this same time every morning, but inwardly Tad convinced himself it was. Emerging from the hedgerow at the Jones' side yard, Tad came out onto Curling Street right as Patty Greene was walking out of her door. Tad slowed to let her catch up, all the while acting like he had not even really noticed her. This was a skill all of those with out-of-their-league crushes eventually adopt.

"Good morning, Patty," he said nervously, making sure to ride on the non-black eye side of her.

"Um hey, Tad, what are you doing here?" she asked, looking around for Luke since the two friends were never apart on their morning commute.

"I thought I would take a new route to school today to break up the boredom," he lied, badly.

"How's the eye," Patty asked, as Tad wished she had not.

"Its fine, look about that, I didn't mean for that to happen, not the black eye, I mean the fight. I really lost my temper," he explained.

"That seems to happen a lot with Chuck," she said understandingly. In that moment Tad Tucker fell just a little bit more, and her smile on this day would stay with him for many years to come, but for now, lost in the moment, Tad was suddenly aware Patty had stopped walking and was asking him a question. He stopped his bike as clarity returned to him, while Patty repeated herself.

"Tad, do you still have it?" she said again, this time with him hearing her.

"Do I still have what?" Tad asked.

"The shoe," she said, "look, I know it's not a Barbie shoe like Chuck said. It's too big. And I have a lot of dolls, Tad, and I've never seen a shoe like that for any of them, so what is it really?" she implored.

"Well, the reason it's not a Barbie shoe is also because I don't play with Barbie dolls," Tad felt he needed to add for the record, "But, no, I don't have it anymore. I don't want to talk about it either, OK?"

"OK," she said, "have it your way."

Inwardly Tad began to question why he had come this way in the first place if not to try and convince Patty that yesterday did not go the way he hoped it would. But the realization she was actually curious about the shoe only after he had given up on it and thrown it away made him upset.

"So, you believe me then, since you know it wasn't a doll shoe?" he asked hopefully.

"Believe you? That it was an Elf shoe? Of course I don't believe that Tad. I said it didn't look like any doll shoe I have seen but that doesn't mean it belonged to some Elf-thing or whatever. I thought you were just trying to make us all laugh," Patty said.

"But Patty, I swear I saw..." Tad started to say but then backed away as Patty was joined by her friends, the gossipy Dowdy girls, Kim and Michelle. They both shot Tad a look like he had no business riding alongside Patty, and she seemed to sense it too, quickly catching up with them and leaving Tad behind. Tad pedaled slowly and hopelessly on as Patty turned to give him an apologetic stare. Her confusedly compassionate look said it all. She felt sorry for him, but also thought he was a huge weirdo. Tad started to think seeing an Elf was the worst thing that ever happened to him.

Meanwhile, on his normal route to school, sans his best friend, Luke Monroe painfully came to a similar conclusion as Chuck Bain and his mob stepped out from behind the dumpster with sneering smiles and fists clenched tight.

12

Following their encounter with the Rack Oon, the first sighting of the Tucker, and the destruction of their means across the ditch, Pedwyn Dale and his fellow Faeries realized their adventure thus far had been a very long one. Their day had started much earlier in Faerie as the time links between their home and the human world did not always mesh. So, while the sun was still in the sky for on what was unknown to them a Tuesday afternoon, their internal body clocks were off to the point they decided it best to make a hidden nest and settle in for the night. Fee the Dink fell asleep first, and her snore eventually lulled everyone else into a peaceful slumber. Even the Rack Oon, though he had no reason to do so, nestled next to the small Faeries and slept through the night.

In the morning, breakfast was made with the stores they had all brought along with them. Everyone prepared and ate a small portion of their food, saving the rest for the unknown. Hetchy devoured all of his at once. Being a tidy sort, they all cleaned up and erased any signs of their meal preparation and campsite. They packed their gear, stretched, and declared themselves ready for the oncoming day.

"Where's Pedwyn?" BeBoo Pevin asked the group. Wippa pointed his spindly arm toward the ditch bank. They all walked over to where he was and stood there for some time watching him, each falling into their own characteristics.

Pedwyn Dale stood looking forlornly at the ruined bridge and the recent rain rushing current of Cooper's Ditch. Arms crossed and chewing on his beard, he was deep in thought and ignoring the impatient mutterings of Wippa, the fact that Hetchy was chewing on a wet stick, Fee's soft cooing, and BeBoo's constant questioning of how they planned to cross the stream.

"Do you have it Wippa?" Pedwyn asked hopefully, "the scent of the Tucker?"

He asked this knowing one of the few strongpoints Wippa's presence brought to the small troop was that Spriggans were renowned for their ability to follow a scent. Getting one to do so was the problem. Wippa spat on the marshy ground, frowned, and yawned, as if answering Pedwyn's plea was the last thing on his mind. Stretching his spindly arms out, and yawning again, he eventually confirmed Pedwyn's hopes.

"Then we shall find a way across this channel, follow the Tucker, and be home well and soon my friends," Pedwyn said with eagerness.

Seeing no clear way across the water became the obvious challenge to Pedwyn's plan. For long hours, the Faeries all searched the ditch bank on their side, hoping to be the one to find the solution. Even Wippa and Hetchy helped, both with their own ulterior motive. Wippa desired to get this over with so he could finally pull a prank on a human. Hetchy was innately curious of the cuisine on the far side of the ditch. Just then, Fee the Dink rose and chirped loudly as the others all stopped what they were doing to look at the small blue Faery. She smiled and flew just off the ground towards the water's edge. The Faeries all went quiet and watched as Fee hovered just above the water, dipping her toes into the stream, searching for the right pitch of melody. Beautiful melodic quirks of sound flowed from the Dink's pursed lips as her tiny arms spun madly about and her flying movements resulted in spins and twists and flips that amounted to a matching dance. Eventually, she settled on a note, singing it pure and lengthy before ending with a sharp buzzing thwip. Before BeBoo could even ask what that was all about - and he was about to ask - bubbles started to form on the distant side of the stream, slowly making their way across the surface. All the Faeries stood silently on the ditch bank while the fizzes approached, rapt with wonder as to what Fee had done to cause this event. The Rack Oon took this opportunity to slip into the reeds and disappear, going unnoticed by the distracted gathering along the water's edge. Even Wippa sat momentarily transfixed along with the rest of them as the ripples first begun by the Dink's wing beats now seemed to grow larger from farther out in the water. Finally, a head broke the water's surface, and two large snapping turtles came plodding out onto the muddy edge of the stream. Without introducing themselves, making eye contact, or even seeming to notice Wippa slowly testing their shells for weaknesses, the turtles sat low and allowed Fee the Dink to climb up on the back of the leader. She turned to Pedwyn with a welcoming smile, and he understood. Their way across was musically provided.

89

"A beautiful song indeed, Miss Fee, "he said, "a beautiful song indeed."

The sunlight licked Pedwyn Dale's exposed smiling cheeks as he turned on the group and motioned for them to all follow him onto the backs of the turtles. The broad, flat, hard-shelled carapaces of the two creatures were amply suited as transport for the little Faeries, and they divided themselves up into two equally weighty parties to be easily carried across the waters of the ditch and deposited safely on the other side. They were all lulled by Fee's soft singing and cooing as the turtles entered the water, staying above the waterline as they safely guided the party across to the far shore. Pedwyn thanked them profusely and the snappers seemed to give him a curtsy nod, but it was Fee who drew their attention and warm meaningful gestures of fondness, so much so that Pedwyn eventually had to pull the Dink away from her admiring duo. She chirped a final thank you to the pair as they sank beneath the waters and the party of Faeries all nodded in Fee's direction in a silent appreciation for her efforts.

Now with two shoes on, Pedwyn Dale set foot on the other side of the stream, excited to think his journey was coming near to an end. He had no way of knowing he was at this point as far removed from the Mists of Faerie as he had ever been, as any of them had ever been. None of them realized they represented the first troop of Faeries, each the first of their species, to truly set foot into the world of the humans for nearly five hundred years. Though denizens of Faerie had graced the

World with their presence countless times in the recent centuries and beyond, they had always stayed within the confines of the Mist-holes and were therefore able to vanish at a moment's notice back to within the Mist between. Now it was different. Now the Faeries with Pedwyn Dale were all on their own, to suffer the trials and hurdles of the human world in an era unknown to all of them. There was no easy way of returning across the water to the Mist-holes, no easy way to hide or counter the dangers they would find in this strange new world, no easy way of completing their task and returning to Hollow Hill having followed the Shee-Queen's direct order and assumption of not being seen. Yet, you would not know it from the looks on their faces. To a Faery, they were wide-eyed and grinning ear to ear - those who possessed ears and mouths with symmetrical combinations that is. All of them were eager and ready to impress along the way in this new adventure, BeBoo Pevin was practically dancing there in the muddy side bank of the ditch. Their journey was just beginning.

Safely across the water, the Faeries scooted up the far bank and received their first view of the new troubles they would face crossing this human world to find the house of the Tucker. Standing amongst tall grasses along a paved roadside, the troop stood in petrified charm as the occasional automobile sped by along Wheeler's Pond Lane towards the town. As the last red speeding object vanished across the crest, Pedwyn turned to his friends and explained the human carriages were unlike any found in their homeland.

"I knew we would see strange things," BeBoo said quietly, "ready to press on here!"

Pedwyn smiled at the courage of the young Pixie and simply nodded his appreciation to him and the others for keeping themselves together thus far.

"I have seen such things before," he began, "Obviously you know I saw the Tucker speed past in his carriage, but I have seen other sites in the World, other things that you must steady yourselves for. The humans... are very busy," he ended.

"How have you seen these things before?" BeBoo asked curiously.

"I know this will come as no surprise to you all, but I am sometimes rather clumsy," Pedwyn said, not expecting anyone to object. None of them did. "I have fallen through before, there was no one around in those places and I stayed long enough to see things before my return. Sometimes I would take rests while picking my elderberries...."

"Probably every hour," BeBoo interrupted.

Pedwyn stopped and was about to reply but before he could, Wippa spat and scratched his claws into the dirt as Fee sang a low note to imply how they all knew Pedwyn slept on his job constantly, and even Hetchy just stared at him daring him to deny the accusation.

"Fine!" Pedwyn hoarsely whispered, "that is not the point. What I was getting at was that I have spent more time in the Mists than any of you and I have seen the Mist-holes open to the World. I suppose, like all of our breed, I am a bit curious as to how things work there, and so I would crawl over and peer through. I have seen the humans, their carriages, their buildings, their....," he paused here, unsure of what to reveal to his now captive audience, and he decided to just leave it at that.

"I KNEW it!" BeBoo said loudly, "you are as excited as the rest of us to be here. Punishment indeed! This is an adventure, and we need to start treating it as one!"

"No," Pedwyn said sharply, "we will no doubt embark on what you could call an adventure, but we are not here to merry ourselves, BeBoo. I have seen the humans at their worst, and there is a reason our laws prevent us from being seen or coming here unwarranted. Things are not as they were in the stories the Nanns still tell. Please, I implore you, let us all be careful."

"You know," BeBoo said, having to get the last word in, "you remind me sometimes of my old Nann." Pedwyn rolled his eyes and turned back to the road.

Pedwyn stood carefully within the tall grass daring to peer out along the roadway to make sure the carriages were gone. Motioning for his fellows to follow, he quickly sped across the roughly paved rural roadway into the safety of the unkept field on the other side. Moving off the road into the seeming

93

safety of the middle ground, the troop stopped to rest, realizing they had not done so at any point since breakfast. Hetchy made it painfully clear he was famished and Pedwyn absentmindedly sent him off in search of food for himself and for the rest of them. Though they had brought various cheeses and stores from their homes, Pedwyn thought it best to save them for times they could not forage from their surroundings. Wippa cleared the ground in the center of the circle where the Faeries sat and using the trickster magic of his kind produced a small spark of fire which ignited the kindling he had gathered. Fee chirped her approval and Pedwyn warned him to guard against too much smoke giving their position away. Wippa frowned and paid little attention to their overly protective leader.

Hetchy returned from his search for food and proudly flopped down a large pile of what he had gathered. The Faeries just stared at him while he unknowingly beamed, expecting their praises. His mound consisted of clumps of sod and reeds, a cicada shell husk, two buttercups, a sprinkle of dandelion seeds, and a few ants who were clearly still alive and trying to escape.

"Pedwyn..." BeBoo started, before Mr. Dale cut him off.

"I know. I know," he said, waving his hand to silence the Pixie so to not upset the Bogie. "Hetchy, my friend, the rest of us discussed it, and we decided we would rather eat our own food this meal and pass this bounty you have found onto you."

"mUwahhh?" the Bogie asked, halfheartedly feigning surprise, but knowing all along he intended to eat most of it all himself anyway. With that he started to devour the things in front of him as various ants ran for the safety of the grass.

After the Faeries had eaten their meals, and Wippa had "accidentally" kicked Hetchy in the back, starting a small tussle that only ended when Fee whistled loudly into their ears, Pedwyn Dale suggested they all get some sleep while he kept watch.

"But Pedwyn," BeBoo started, "it is still daylight, and we are just starting out!" His excitement at seeing more of the World was welling up inside him to dangerous levels.

"This I know, little one, but listen, we should travel in the dark, and we need to be well rested to do so," Pedwyn said.

Sadly for BeBoo, this made too much sense, and the others took the order as an opportunity to curl up and get a few hours rest before dark. They all drifted off to sleep as Pedwyn Dale sat by the dying embers and kept watch. The soft perfectly pitched snoring of Fee the Dink kept them all in a beautiful slumber and their guardian actually stayed up a few minutes into his watch before he rolled over asleep, beard in mouth.

13

Tad took his seat and waited for Luke. His friend was always on time, early even, so as to avoid Chuck in the hallway. Yet, as the class slowly filled with students, Luke's chair remained empty. Tad turned to risk giving Chuck Bain a glance, but his nemesis only smiled at him. Turning back, Tad was relieved to see Luke slowly come into the classroom however, his relief turned to shame when he saw his friend's swollen bottom lip with drying blood. Tad turned to give Chuck a scowl, but the bully was not focusing on him, instead whispering little tales into the ears of those next to him who found this whole affair comical. Tad started to say something when the teacher came into the classroom demanding the students' attention. He hoped Luke would speak up and reveal to her the cause of his bloody lip, but his friend kept silent, never once looking in Tad's direction.

The day dragged slowly by until lunch. Tad hustled through the halls to seat himself at the usual table with Luke and their friends, but was surprised to see Luke sit himself at a different table in the corner of the lunchroom. Tad slowly walked over and sat silently across from Luke, his friend turning in his seat to avoid Tad's gaze.

"Luke," Tad asked, "why aren't you talking to me?"

"Leave me alone, Tad," his friend replied, "I don't want to talk about it OK?"

"Luke, I'm sorry I didn't meet you this morning, I had..."

"It's not just that Tad, it's not just Chuck, it's all of them, they are all laughing at us, talking about us. You had to drag me into this Elf thing when I asked you not to. It is hard enough being at this school and just trying to get through a normal day without all this added to it. I am not ready for my test. I have to explain to my mom what happened to my lip. I have to stop hanging out, Tad, this was fun for a while, but I can't keep playing make believe."

"Make believe?" Tad asked incredulously, "but you said you believed me."

"I'm not sure I ever said I really believed you, Tad" said Luke, "you just dragged me into it so fast. I just went along with it, but this is too far. I don't think we can hang out anymore, Tad," his friend said defiantly.

"But we are best frien..." Tad started to say before noticing how Luke was looking around at others watching their conversation and trying to act as if he were not really talking to Tad. "You know what, Luke?" Tad said, "have it your way, go take your stupid math test. I don't want to be your friend anymore anyway!"

Tad stood up and pushed his chair away from the table with force. Luke watched him walk away and sadly returned to eating his lunch alone. Tad turned the corner, holding back tears of anger, frustration, and sadness. His one ally and best friend was not willing to put up with the downside of being friends with the boy who saw the Elf. No one believed him, they were all laughing at him behind his back, and he was beginning to realize the problems brought about by this whole affair. There in the hallway, crouching down, he started to consider never speaking or thinking of any of this again. But then Tad's resolve hardened. He took the time to let his mind remember the details. The dirty white torn and tattered shirt, the drooping red hat, the black leather shoes, and the look. The look on the little man's wrinkled face.

"That was no doll," Tad said to himself in bold reassurance. "I know what I saw. I am NOT making this up!" "I know no one will believe me until I finally prove it somehow."

"Are you actually talking to yourself?" Patty Greene asked in disbelief, having stopped while walking past. The Dowdy girls began to giggle and whisper. Tad looked around desperately for someone else nearby he could claim he was speaking with, but it was obvious he was caught. He looked up sheepishly and just shrugged. Patty turned to her giggling friends and joined in their laughter as they disappeared around the corner.

"HOW could this get ANY worse?!" Tad pondered, once again speaking out loud to himself. Standing up, he began to hastily make for his locker before the bell rang signaling a return to class. As if in answer to his spoken question, cruel fate chose that moment for Chuck Bain to head for his locker too, which was right across the hall from Tad's.

"Well, well," Chuck sneered, "look who we have here, guys, it's Doll-Boy himself, the great Elffo!" Chuck Bain's hyena-like friends laughed with guttural sounds and motions.

"Don't call me that!" Tad resounded, "It was NOT a doll!"

"Oh, OK...so it was an ELF then? Chuck asked mockingly, "That's what you're going to stand by? You seriously think you saw an Elf? Oh Man, Tucker, I used to not like you, but now I think I'm actually a little worried about you," Chuck said, sounding suddenly serious in a deceiving way, "I think from now on we will just give you your space and leave you alone..."

Tad was about to actually respond to Chuck with relief, having momentarily believed the bully was sincere about leaving him alone finally. But before he could get the words out, Chuck finished his sentence.

"....besides, Luke is so much easier to beat up anyway!" Chuck laughed.

"You leave him alone!" Tad said, defending his friend and surprisingly pushing Chuck back toward the lockers. Chuck stumbled backwards with surprise before catching himself. Chuck reacted with expectations, swinging at Tad with his hardened fist. The blow did not connect and before another

100

could be swung, both boys were being held fast by teachers and once again on their way to the Principal's office.

14

The streetlight crackled and buzzed, gradually illuminating the side street to signify the approaching dusk. Pedwyn Dale momentarily looked up in wonder at the plastic-covered glow of the bulb before signaling the small troop quickly across the road, down into a shallow boundary ditch, and up again into the well-kept grass yard fronting the large brick home of some Worldly resident. The Faerie gang nestled beneath a large well-groomed hedge row, while Pedwyn conducted a head count.

"Is everyone here?" he asked hopefully, noticing how Hetchy had been purposely straying behind and looking for things to eat, or expel things he had eaten along the way, and sometimes casually re-eat them.

"Present and accounted for!" BeBoo exhaled, his excitement at running across the landscape thus far palpable.

From Wheeler's Pond Lane, the Faeries had made steady progress through unkept and unwatched fields, a smaller low water-filled ditch, down a dusty dirt backroad, and finally across the newly-laid parking lot for what would become the next Saves-So-Big Shopping Center. Here the trail Wippa was sensing suddenly became cold, until he eventually ascertained the boys had jumped their bikes over a small culvert and cut through a corridor between fenced-in back yards to emerge onto another dimly-lit street leading into something called Shady

Glen Estates. Here the group found itself beneath the hedge in the first yard of what was apparently the neighborhood of the Tucker.

"Do you still have it?" Pedwyn inquired of Wippa. The Spriggan hissed sharply, signifying he was skilled at his tracking and weary of being asked. Wippa haphazardly motioned across the yard with an extended boney finger, intent on providing Pedwyn with the direction but not telling him how far it might be or how strong the scent still carried. Wippa knew the boys had passed near here the prior day. Pedwyn sighed and peered out from below the hedge to slink across the low grass yard. It was then he saw the dog.

The animal was watching them with mild curiosity and began a series of muffled barks to let them know he was aware of their presence in his yard. Pedwyn froze. BeBoo peered from behind him curiously.

"What is it, Pedwyn? Is it friendly like the Rack Oon?" Slowly the Pixie began to adjust his Star-Hat until Pedwyn reached down to grab his shoulder and steady him.

"Careful, do not make any sudden movements" he pleaded, really having no idea what to do next. The dog watched them with mounting interest and took an initial step towards the gathering, causing the Faeries to collectively step back. Suddenly, a light came on from the front porch of the brick home. A human opened a front door and yelled out:

"Bob Barker! Hurry boy! Do your business and get back in here!"

The dog turned to look at the human by the front door, and the training of having been through this ordeal countless times in his life began to kick in. Ignoring the strange creatures to his left, and having no regard for his own privacy, Bob Barker did his business. The Faeries blanched in horror as they watched the animal adjust itself on its haunches and lift up its backside.

"Is he about to..." BeBoo asked before his question was answered.

Fee the Dink let slip a low-rolling peal to show her displeasure and embarrassment for the situation in which they found themselves involved. The others all coiled at the sounds and smells and tried to look away. Wippa however had to look back in mild admiration at the size of the spoil.

Just then the Faeries heard a gaudy, gushing vomit and turned swiftly to see Hetchy heaving up his recent repast. Having viewed the current event, he was abruptly aware of what he had prior discovered and eaten as they crossed the side yard - last night's business. Puking and twitching across the grass, Pedwyn became concerned Hetchy was going to cause the human in the house to hear them and investigate. Pedwyn began to panic. Turning to and from his position he noticed a large, brown, oblong-shaped leather stringed object lying beneath a small shrub in front of the house.

"BeBoo, your Glee-Wand!" he exclaimed, not believing he was encouraging the Pixie to use this unwieldy magic item. He pointed to the odd ball-like object, and BeBoo immediately went into action. The Pixie extricated the Glee-Wand from wherever it was he kept it and waved it at the leather ball. The ball levitated slightly then spiraled towards Hetchy at rapid speed as BeBoo directed it. Hetchy barely had time to adjust his mouth to catch the object, enlarge his jaws as his species are capable of, and completely engulf the ball in his maw to help divest himself of the taste of Bob Barker's leavings. Somewhere in the far back rows of his sharpened teeth, his new meal was punctured and popped. The Faeries, and a still straining Bob Barker, watched as Hetchy's cheeks extended and his eyes bulged. He kept the ball inside his teeth in an amazing effort to hold onto his food. His eyes and face swelled to four times their size and this sight spooked the dog so much he quickly finished his duty and ran whimpering to the front porch. The next night, unbeknownst to the Faeries, Bob Barker would refuse to go outside and instead do his business on the living room carpet. The humans would not be pleased.

BeBoo let out a soft whistle and holstered his Glee-Wand - somewhere. Pedwyn waited for the front porch light to go out and then quickly led the Faerie friends across the front yard and across several lawns without further incident.

Wippa continued to track the trail of the Tucker, momentarily distracted by the trace of what he concluded was the other human boy-child turning on another course. As the moon hung low, the Spriggan led the Fae through taller grass and stealthily along a sunken flower bed until arriving at a metal chain-link fence. There beneath the flowers and light brush, he pointed to the side window where a faint glow shone from behind yellowish curtains. Pedwyn motioned for Fee, and she took the cue to scout ahead. Hovering up and easily through the chain-link fence, Fee flew flittingly onward towards the lit window. She soundlessly perched on a brick ledge and stood on stretched out tip-toes to peek inside. Fee turned back to her friends with a twinkle in her small dotted eyes and risked a flirty whistle which signaled to Pedwyn they had lastly arrived at their location. Pedwyn turned to Wippa and risked petting him behind his sharp ears, for a brief second the Spriggan allowed this before he abruptly hissed and poked Pedwyn's hand away.

"Very well done indeed, my friend Wippa," Pedwyn beamed, "very well done indeed!"

The Spriggan attempted a convivial smile, but his kind are more natural to sneers and the attempt was rather awkward and in a small way terrifying. Pedwyn returned a smile, nevertheless.

They waited for the clouds to silently cover the new moon glow before squeezing through the fence links each in their own way, some sliding through easily, others contorting their bodies in ways only akin to their species. They made use of the trellis aside the lit window to quickly join Fee the Dink along the brick ledge. Five sets of Faerie eyes finally gazed into the house of the Tucker.

15

Tad sat miserably at the kitchen table, two letters from the Principal spread out before him along with a disastrous test result from an exam he neglected to study for while searching for his Elf. His parents stood over him with fuming expressions and arms folded. The argument and strain they had manufactured between each other only an hour prior was now redirected toward him. Tad had been given the standard "*wait until your father gets home*" speech from his mother the entire drive home after the school called to notify her to pick him up following another scuffle. He had sulked in his room until the streetlights came on signaling his father's arrival home from work was nearing. He expected his parents' call soon after his father came in the door, but they had to get their own tensions out of the way first, and he was almost briefly thankful for their hostility toward one another as it delayed his inevitable scolding. Erin sat forgotten in her room, listening to all the shouting from her mother to her brother, then between her parents, and finally for her brother to come down and face his music. Her stomach grumbled as dinner seemed to take forever. Her birthday being the following day should have consumed her child thoughts, but it was sadly not on her mind as she finally braved to open her bedroom door and tiptoe down the stairs, pulled along by the delightful smell of lasagna baking.

Erin quietly sat at the table as her father was scribbling his signature on Tad's disciplinary notes and failing test grade.

Her mother mumbled something about having him sign some other papers later, and he looked up at her with an angry scoff.

"Really?" he said in disbelief, "you have to bring that up here now?"

"I think we have put it off long enough," her mother said quietly. Erin was about to ask what papers, but Tad wisely kicked her beneath the table and shook his head. She took the message to mean she should not ask, so she did not.

Her father sat sullenly at the table, not asking her how her day was at school, not asking if she were excited about her birthday, or even looking in her direction. Erin sank into a silent pout. Her brother joined her in unspoken brooding.

"Um, so the lasagna is not ready yet," their mother said embarrassingly. Her preparation of papers for her husband, and her distraction by Tad's trouble at school, had preoccupied her from putting the meal in at the required time in order for it to be ready once the family sat down for dinner. The piping hot lasagna needed a few more minutes to cool down on the kitchen counter. She had also been distracted by the early baking of Erin's cake, which also sat cooling on the counter, its thick layer of vanilla frosting still in need of decoration.

"Typical," Ronald Tucker mumbled under his breath.

Tad looked up for his mother's expected retort and she was about to deliver one, when a sharp, piercing, melodic whistle sounded from outside the window. Helen turned to the screen, followed by the eyes of her husband and children.

"What was that, mom?" Erin asked, "it sounded like a pretty bird!"

"Rather late for a bird to be out chirping like that," her father answered, "but I suppose it was. Either that or some insect. Pretty sound though, wasn't it?"

Fee the Dink overheard this human compliment and smiled coyly to herself as Pedwyn softly patted her tiny blue head. Pedwyn and the Faeries had moved quickly when the family turned to look out the window, but slowly began to emerge back upon the brick ledge and peer into the glass. There they saw their Pixie friend smiling and signaling them from behind a large cookie jar. Hetchy stood on his tip toes to see better and hoped BeBoo brought him a cookie, or three. BeBoo had dropped from the ceiling vent, slipped down the kitchen wall, and hid behind the large container. He opened Pedwyn's leafy wrapping he had been given, and with the risky magic of his Glee-Wand, sprinkled its contents evenly across the family meal, before once again disappearing behind a large black heat-producing apparatus.

"A most welcome distraction indeed, Miss Fee, a most welcome distraction," Pedwyn beamed as he continued to caress the proud Dink. He knew soon the Tucker would consume his family meal, and unknowingly with it the Mooncheese, forgetting ever seeing Pedwyn Dale and allowing him and his companions

113

to triumphantly return to Hollow Hill. Their reluctant adventure was nearing its end, he thought.

BeBoo continued to hide in the human kitchen, while the mother eventually served the family meal. She cut the lasagna into portions and gave each family member a healthy slice. Watching from the window, and from behind the cookie jar, the Faeries stared in eagerness waiting for the Tucker to eat the Mooncheese-laced food. Tad absentmindedly pulled his bread apart and halfheartedly chewed on a piece. Hetchy drooled from the window ledge.

"So, tell me about these fights," Tad's father asked in an effort to bring up something to break the tension of knowing his wife had divorce papers ready in the other room.

"It was nothing really, we just fought," Tad answered without giving anything away initially, "Twice," he added in an embarrassed whisper.

"Tad, you tell us right now what you boys were fighting about, this is not like you, none of this is, bad grades, trouble at school, what is going on with you?" his mother asked, with clear agitation in her already troubled voice. Erin sat quietly, wondering why no one was asking her what she wanted on her birthday cake.

"I got in fights because the kids at school were all making fun of me, OK," Tad finally answered with a little bit of anger. "No one believes me at school, just like no one believes me here, so what's new?" he finished. His parents looked at him and at each other briefly, quizzically.

"What are you talking about? Believe you about what?" his father asked.

"I told you what I saw!" Tad yelled, and realized he was probably raising his voice too loudly, but he was beyond reasoning at this point. "You didn't even listen to me! You didn't ask me anything about it, or turn around when I asked. You haven't asked me anything about it since. So, I know you didn't believe me, no one does!" he screamed.

"Thaddeus!" his mother said sternly, "what are you talking about? Believe you about what?" she asked.

"The little man I saw! I TOLD you! He was an Elf, I think. I TOLD you I saw him!" Tad yelled.

"You saw an Elf?" Erin asked.

"I told YOU, too!" he yelled at her, getting yelled back at by his mother for raising his voice at the table and at his sister. From behind the cookie jar, BeBoo held his ears, and gave a condescending look toward his "Elf" friend in the window.

"He thinks I'm an Elf!" Pedwyn said, rather proud to be mistaken for such a magical Faerie creature. Wippa pinched him behind his knee and hissed.

"Ouch! Fine, but I doubt anyone will ever mistake you for an Elf, my Spriggan friend," he said non-apologetically. Wippa hissed again.

The gathered Faeries turned back to peer inside the window in hopes of watching the Tucker finally eat his meal. From behind the cookie jar, BeBoo extracted his See-Scope from its unknown place of concealment. He stretched out the small spyglass and from his hidden position sent the See-Scope tendril up and around the inner lip of the cookie jar lid. It wound itself snakelike beneath the seal, stopping when the family came into view. From his position, BeBoo could see and hear everything. Unfortunately, for the Faeries' plan, he could also smell everything. He turned his gaze briefly from his See-Scope to find out where the pleasant aroma was coming from, and there he spied the cooling cake only inches from his concealment. A smile spread across his face as a dreamlike trance overcame him. He silently recoiled the See-Scope and almost floated out from behind the cookie jar toward the white-iced cake.

"Oh no," Pedwyn said, almost in an expected tone. He himself had spied the cake and its proximity to the Pixie, and realized the potential for everything to go awry. He was not wrong.

BeBoo Pevin loved cake. To say he loved cake is an understatement. There were long stretches of his life where he basically subsisted on cake. Honey-cakes baked by the Elves with dew-dropped icing and bee-kissed dollops of crème were his favorite. But he was also partial to Dinkybons and Sprite Sprinkles. Every November Eve, the Bullbeggar of Creech Hill would set aside its malevolent ways to bake a batch of small grit-cakes for its neighbors. Though the Pixies and the Bullbeggars never got on well, and in truth no one ever got on well with the Bullbeggars, and certainly not the one from Creech Hill; BeBoo Pevin was almost always first in line. The Bullbeggar usually allowed him to take two, and for that reason alone, BeBoo was always silent when the others talked about the creature behind its back. BeBoo Pevin absolutely loved cake. However, as we shall see, actually eating the cakes was his secondary preference.

"Are you two just going to stare at your dinner?" their mother asked irritably. Ronald Tucker ate his meal in silence, his wife joining him, while their two children sat staring at their plates. Tad sat idly stirring the cheese with his fork while Erin nibbled on her bread holding back tears over the building tension between her brother and her parents.

During this conversation, BeBoo Pevin could no longer contain himself. Only half-concerned about the family sitting in plain view across the room, the Pixie slid across the counter. Pedwyn watched with nervous anticipation until the Pixie again hid behind the large cake.

"No, Mr. Pevin, please no, please do not do it!" Pedwyn nervously exclaimed to himself from outside the window. His companions crowded around him in silence and watched over

117

his shoulders. They were all aware of what was about to happen. That BeBoo Pevin was going to scoop his fingers across the large human cake was a given. He did this finger scooping act more than a few times, voraciously licking the frosting off his minty green digits.

"Tad," his mother said sternly, "eat your dinner please and tell us that you intend to tell your teacher you were making all this Elf stuff up and let things go back to normal, please."

Tad stood and walked over to the counter to refill his glass. He slowly poured his tea and returned to his seat never noticing a small, green creature ducking behind his sister's birthday cake.

"Yeah, like anything has been normal around here in months," he said flippantly.

"Thaddeus!" his mother said crossly, and then she just stopped short, realizing her son was well aware of the things they were trying to keep from him. Tad sat back down and continued staring at his meal, absentmindedly moving pieces around his plate. Helen realized the tensions between her and her husband were affecting their children, and she rashly decided to switch the subject to change the mood. She brought up Erin's birthday causing her daughter to perk up. She asked Erin if she were excited, and then reminded herself to check on the cake.

During this heated exchange between the family, the Faeries' heads turned back and forth with eyes on their Pixie friend and waiting to watch the Tucker finally eat his

Mooncheesey dinner. Hetchy took a few seconds to adjust his eyes so far apart he no longer needed to turn his head.

In this moment, BeBoo Pevin sprang up and landed atop Erin Tucker's birthday cake. Pedwyn gasped. Fee the Dink risked a shrill note of disbelief. Wippa smirked with glee at the assumption everything was about to turn sour. Hetchy caught an unlucky moth who flew by the window to see what the fuss was about. He was almost about to let it go free when his genera instincts got the better of him. He ate it in one savoring bite. They all continued to watch as their fellow Faerie friend ascended the cake and stood upon its center. BeBoo Pevin stood tall, as tall as he could manage, with outstretched arms, legs straight together, and a beaming smile. He slowly bowed low and proud in a gesture that bespoke he was about to perform some regal act or recite some prophetic prose. Instead, he began to dance like his feet were on fire. The Pixie began with stomping his feet up and down and bending his arms in alternating manner, a quirky jerk of motion that made Fee giggle and Pedwyn bury his face in his hands. The Pixie turned to and fro, leaping on frothy bubbles of icing and kicked-up cake. He whirled, he flipped, he spun in a circle while stamping his foot in all directions. He simply lost all control. Had the humans looked toward the counter their worlds would have changed. But the growing argument had them thankfully distracted. And BeBoo Pevin danced on.

Meanwhile on the ledge, Pedwyn raised his head from his hands.

119

"Goodness me is he still doing it?" he asked expectedly. His answer came when he saw BeBoo actually coming to his senses and slowing down, but continuing to make sure he danced on every single inch of the cake top first. Though Pedwyn was upset, mad at himself for not predicting this, and terrified the family would catch his friend, he was not altogether surprised. He turned to Wippa and declared the obvious.

"Pixies dance on cakes," he stated. The Spriggan simply shrugged like Pedwyn was not telling him anything he did not already know. They both turned back to the scene and were thankful to see BeBoo Pevin was no longer in sight, having climbed back down and disappeared somewhere on the kitchen countertop.

In that moment Helen Tucker arose to check on her daughter's cake. She stood over the sweet silently, in disbelief at first, then with a welling anger fueled by the escalating tension in the room. There, on her freshly baked dessert, were hundreds of tiny footprints. There were ninety-eight to be exact, but Helen Tucker was not counting, she was screaming.

"Thaddeus Tucker!" she yelled, "what is the meaning of this?!" Her question was direct and stern and the clear anger in her voice made everyone turn and look. She tilted the cake so that all could see. The top of the icing was covered in small footprints and ruts. BeBoo crouched low.

"I didn't do that!" Tad yelled, pushing his chair back from the table and coming over to have a closer look.

"Did he ruin my cake, mom?!" Erin cried from the table.

"No, honey, don't you worry about this. I can smooth it back down easily, but I want to know why your brother would do something like this! Trying to sell your silly Elf story by ruining your sister's cake with fake footprints. What did you use? Better not have been your fingers!" Helen Tucker was livid, throwing accusations out in anger, and shaking. Her husband tried to calm her down, and the look she gave him made him redirect toward his son.

"Seriously, Tad, this is that Elf business still?" he asked with an unhappy tone.

"I did not do that!" Tad yelled, getting closer and looking at the details of the small prints with what looked like four tiny toe impressions.

"It had to have been him!" he said in a moment of actual hope that his parents would finally believe him. This did not have the desired effect. In that moment Erin began to cry over her ruined cake, his mother was so upset she had to put the cake down for fear of throwing it across the room, and his father was trying to wrap his head around it all.

"There is no Elf, Tad! You did this when you got up to get your tea, now admit it!" his father yelled loudly trying to end the matter.

"I did NOT do this, and I will NOT admit to it! You guys never believe anything I say!" Tad Tucker yelled with welling tears filling his eyes.

"That's it!" his father shouted, "go to your room right now! I don't want to hear another word out of you. I will be up later to discuss this."

"Fine!" Tad said sternly, pushing his chair quickly toward the table and stomping away. Erin watched with gushing tears and asked to be excused, too. Her parents just nodded as she slid from the table and up the stairs.

16

Wippa's spindly thorny fingers easily found the crevices in the mortar and brick wall. The spikey appendages Spriggans called toes were equally adept at attaching themselves in the smallest of cracks, which allowed him to easily climb the surface of the Tucker house from the kitchen window, up and around to the panes on the front of the home. The troop had observed the Tucker children ascend their staircase and correctly guessed their rooms were located on the second level of the building. Wippa risked a low whistle to alert the others to follow him. While the Spriggan possessed the ability to easily scale most any surface, Pedwyn and Hetchy were not altogether unskilled in such endeavors. Albeit much slower, each ultimately made their way up the brick wall and around to the front ledge of Tad Tucker's bedroom window. Fee the Dink simply flew around them teasingly chirping and making sure they did not fall, which Pedwyn almost did, several times.

Tad Tucker was already in his bed, a small lamp shining from his nightstand next to a stack of comic books. He was leaning back on his pillow and the look on his face was one of sad confusion.

"I know what I saw," he said to himself. "I know I found that shoe. I know it smelled too!" He continued laying out all the facts of his prior findings. Pedwyn looked down briefly at his feet when he heard this and reminded himself how he might want to wash his socks in the stream when he arrived back home.

"And I know that I did NOT put any little footprints on Erin's cake!" he said defiantly and, in the moment, convinced himself he was perhaps not crazy after all, and something weird was really happening here. "I am NOT crazy!" he finally said, before realizing how once again he was talking out loud to himself and Patty might have been right to give him an odd look when she caught him doing it last time. He smiled briefly, intent on telling Luke about the footprints the next day and wondering how to set an Elf trap. Just then he heard his father's heavy walk coming up the stairs. Tad braced himself for the imminent scolding, but his parent never entered the room. Instead, he could hear his father softly humming to himself as he bypassed Tad's door and continued down the hall toward his own bedroom. Tad counted his blessings that perhaps his father had not noticed the light and assumed his son had fallen asleep. Tad supposed he could count on his lecture in the morning. Though his empty stomach reminded him of his parent's punishment, he eventually turned out his lamp, fluffed his pillow, and let sleep come over him. As he dreamt boyish dreams, he was entirely unaware of the Spriggan descending silently from his vent and crawling deliberately across his bedroom floor.

Moments earlier, the Faerie troop argued their next move on the window ledge. Pedwyn was coming up with numerous unsound plans, but the others were only halfheartedly listening. Being troop Faeries, they were somewhat tidy, and expected the human home to be in what they considered "apple-pie order." However, this was the first time any of their kind had seen the inside of a ten-year-old human boy's bedroom. Tad Tucker's room was a complete mess. Growing weary of having to peer inside and look at this carnage, Wippa finally hissed his idea, and the others could simply find no objection. The Spriggan would gain entry, traverse the Tucker's floor, climb onto the bed, and just cram his Mooncheese down the boy's throat. Pedwyn ultimately agreed they should have thought of this to begin with, but warned Wippa not to shove the cheese too hard and harm the child. Wippa merely smirked eerily and acquiesced, though he secretly planned to "accidentally" scratch the boy.

Wippa had entered the Tucker home through the vent system, and made his way through the aluminum maze using his nose, which by now had memorized Tad Tucker's scent. As the child slept, the Spriggan ultimately made it onto the floor beneath a wooden desk opposite the bed. Wippa's sharp orangish eyes peered out from below the desk and ascertained the location best suitable to ascend onto the bed. He took great delight in being the one to accomplish this mission and get them all back home. Though he was having some fun in the World, he was mostly bored due to constantly being kept in check by Pedwyn Dale. This would be his shining moment.

Pedwyn and the others watched from the window as their Spriggan companion crept from the desk and across the floor towards the slumbering Tucker. He darted from a heap of

125

clothes to a stack of books, then a pile of plastic building blocks, and ultimately to the foot stand of the boy's bed. From the window, Fee the Dink fluttered about buzzing with excitement. Pedwyn watched wide-eyed in hopes this was finally going to be it, and Hetchy was actually momentarily observant, mostly due to having nothing to currently eat. They were all waiting anxiously, but the Spriggan seemed frozen in place. They continued to wait, nearly holding their breath, but Wippa sat still, unmoving.

"Goodness me, what is he waiting for?" Pedwyn asked the others, but no one could answer. The Spriggan sat, looking about in confusion, making only slight efforts to even lift his arms up at the wooden bed leg before rapidly bringing them back down.

"Something is wrong," Pedwyn stated. He waved his hands frantically in an attempt to get the Spriggan to notice him. Eventually he gave up, and just continued to watch in hopes Wippa would regroup and accomplish his mission. Wippa disappeared around the opposite side of the bed, and Pedwyn sighed in relief thinking the Spriggan was merely finding the best point of ascent. However, he was again disappointed to see Wippa appear in the same spot, looking up at the window with shrugging shoulders. Pedwyn frantically pointed at the Spriggan, and then to Tad Tucker atop the bed, motioning for Wippa to get on with it. Wippa turned one more time to the bed, then turned back to his friends on the sill, and retched.

126

"Barrrrffffft," Hetchy giggled from the ledge, assuming his friend was merely making room for something he found in there he wanted to eat.

"Goodness me!" Pedwyn gasped as he watched the Spriggan slide one of Tad Tucker's shoes across the floor and rub it over the leavings he had expelled onto the carpet.

"Goodness me!" he said again, "What has gotten into him, or better yet what has come out of him? What is going on?" he asked in desperation as he watched the Spriggan defeatedly climb back up the wall and ultimately out the vent system and back towards the ledge. Wippa continued down the brick wall and crawled beneath a bush underneath a lower level window. His friends followed, and Pedwyn pressed him for what had gone wrong. Wippa looked at him in a miserably forlorn way and hissed sharply and accusingly. Pedwyn interpreted the Spriggan's hiss and slapped his hands onto his forehead. He took a big breath and admitted he should have realized their plan was too simple.

"A sock," he told the others, "the Tucker has a sock under his bed."

Wippa hissed again. Pedwyn nodded and added detail to his interpretation.

"A dirty sock," he said. Fee chirped a low frowning boo sound.

They were all aware of the poignancy of the Spriggan ability to track smells, this would have only amplified the stench of the human child's filthy sock. None of them could imagine the reek as it assailed Wippa's extended nostrils. But the smell is not what held the Spriggan back. He was after all acclimated by then to the nauseating smell of Pedwyn Dale's dirty socks and shoes. But they were properly on his feet where they belonged.

Somewhere in their collective histories, humans and Fae somewhat coinhabited certain friendlier places. Even then there were some who discounted such things, but most could explain away their human foibles by blaming it on the Wee Folk. For example, if one had knots in their hair, it was not because they were not overly fond of washing it, but due to the trickster Faeries tying their locks in clusters while they slept. Milk was prematurely spoiled, crops blighted, and various other pranks were pulled by the giggling Little People. Eventually, the country folk grew wary of this chicanery and began to develop methods to thwart their little neighbors troublesome attentions. Most of these remedies were discovered quite by accident. But once they were proven, the rumors spread from village to town and ultimately became well-known and utilized much to the Faeries' chagrin. Most of these home-grown methods for Faerie wards were long forgotten, and even if he knew of them, Tad Tucker would have had limited access to ancient church mold or St. John's Wort. What he did have, like ancient county folk in Wales discovered centuries ago, was what every boy his age possessed, a misplaced unclean sock under his bed. A knife under his pillow would have sufficed. So too, a twig of broom, a pig's head, or flax upon his floor. But Tad Tucker slept on, unknowing that his lost sock protected his memory for one more night.

Pedwyn hung his head, and patted Wippa measuredly to let him know the blame was not his. None of them could have been able to ascend the bed knowing a single sock was beneath. It was simply impossible for their kind to accept such a travesty of laundry or misplaced cloth. Pedwyn realized it was too good to be true to assume they could just put the cheese into the Tucker's mouth. No, he would have to resort once again to stealth and a good plan. Just then he realized something and gasped.

"Goodness me," he whispered sharply, "where's the Pixie?"

17

Helen Tucker put away her children's untouched meals and cleared the remainder of the family's dinner from the table. Once everything was in order, she poured herself a small glass of wine, tuned the radio to her favorite station, and began to hum along as she repaired the icing on her daughter's cake. As she did this, smoothing out the imperfections and making the icing flat again, she was unaware of the sizeable missing chunk of cake that BeBoo Pevin had gorged himself on. The Pixie had simply crammed his hands into the side wall of the cake, eating as much of it as he could stuff into his mouth before mending his obvious intrusion with extra icing from the cake's bottom, which he then hungrily licked off his fingers. Once she had resurfaced the cake icing, she began to squeeze out decorations, creating red roses of frosting with a cursive script that read:

Happy 7ᵗʰ Birthday Erin!!

BeBoo Pevin hid behind the cookie jar and kept quiet. He continued to watch as the Tucker mother finished with the cake, and unfortunately for him, placed it inside a plastic covering and into the large refrigerator along with the family's uneaten meal. She then got out various meats, cheeses, fruits and snacks, from both the refrigerator and the cabinet, and placed them upon the counter. BeBoo held his breath as she reached for the cookie jar where he was hiding, but she opened it and removed the treats without ever noticing his green figure in the kitchen's half-light. She laid out all the food and began to prepare her children's lunches. She retrieved from a drawer a brown paper bag for Tad, and from the cabinet above, a soft pink Strawberry Shortcake lunchbox for Erin. She set out the bread in front of each child's container, placed meat and cheese upon the slices, and turned ever so briefly to get plastic bags for the pending sandwiches. In these seconds, true to his species reputation for quick thinking, BeBoo Pevin acted. When Helen Tucker turned back around, she had no notice of her son's sandwich containing an extra slice of cheese.

Helen Tucker finished packing her children's lunches and placed them into the refrigerator to keep until the morning. She continued to softly hum to herself and seemed lost in thought as she put away the last of the dishes and cleaned the crumbs off the counter. She gave the kitchen one last visual inspection before turning out the light and walking upstairs. BeBoo Pevin waited for the echo of her footsteps to fade before extracting himself from behind the microwave. He was chagrined by the missing cake but told himself he could not have eaten another bite, though in truth he probably would have. Eventually, he returned to the vent system and crawled through the maze back outside the house where he searched for his companions. Seeing they were no longer on the window ledge, he briefly panicked, before realizing he was alone in the World without Pedwyn Dale to temper his exploration. He found a spot beneath a small bush and gave one last look around for his friends. Still not seeing them, he decided it was time to look from a higher vantage point. BeBoo Pevin donned his Star-Hat.

The small woolen hat began to glow slightly when the Pixie placed it on his head. The star map looked slightly different in Faerie, so the Star-Hat needed a small amount of adjustment time. Once its' bearings were clear, the hat turned into an inky blackness with small pricks of white light which perfectly mirrored the current stars in the sky above. This same magic eventually encompassed the wearer and as it lifted him towards the sky, he became impossible to distinguish from the canopy of constellations. Up and up the Star-Hat carried BeBoo Pevin until he mentally commanded it to halt. From his current position he could see the entirety of the Tucker's street, neighborhood, and most of the surrounding town. The Pixie was marveled by the enormity of the sight, and the number of streetlights, roadways, homes, buildings, and off in the far distance, a woodland of enormous trees. He thought to himself it would take a long time to fully explore all of this and set about making a mental list of where to start before he heard the soft booing whistle of Fee the Dink from below.

BeBoo guided the Star-Hat to the upper window ledge where he finally saw his companions. He briefly hovered above them as Pedwyn was patting Wippa's head for some reason and he was a little surprised the Spriggan had not bitten him yet. As he slowly descended lower, he heard Pedwyn Dale's exasperated query.

133

"I'm right here!" he said excitedly, forgetting his friends could not see him camouflaged against the night sky.

Pedwyn startled so quickly he slipped and was about to fall off the ledge before Wippa nonchalantly, and borderline reluctantly, reached out and grabbed him to pull him back. The surprised Faerie troop began to look all around for where their friends voice had originated.

"BeBoo Pevin!" Pedwyn whispered sharply, "Is that you? Where are you?!"

"I am right HERE!" the Pixie repeated, still forgetting he was undetectable to their eyes. "I am wearing my Star-Hat," he said proudly.

"Well take it off!" Pedwyn whispered, "We cannot see you with that confounded cap on."

"You cannot take a Star-Hat off while you're wearing it Pedwyn," BeBoo said matter of factly. "Everyone knows that" he finished.

Pedwyn chewed on his beard and pondered this. Hetchy watched wishing he had a beard to chew on, or anything. The others waited for Pedwyn to digest this information. He pretended that he did know about Star-Hats, but in reality, he had never really paid them any attention.

"Goodness me that makes no sense, how would you EVER take it off then?" he asked confused. Wippa smacked his forehead. Fee flew low and quiet.

"You cannot take it off while you're in the AIR I mean, silly. I would fall, like a shooting star I suppose," BeBoo answered.

"Well goodness me, why didn't you specify that! Fly down there and hide, we will climb down and meet you," he said this indicating the bush they had gathered at previously and just assumed BeBoo was somewhere he could see where he was pointing.

BeBoo descended with the Star-Hat and waited for his friends to come down from the ledge. Once they arrived, he removed the magic cap and bowed low. Pedwyn rolled his eyes and asked how he came to be floating in the sky next to them. BeBoo related his story to them all, while they told theirs to him. He nodded his head in understanding about the perils of dirty socks, and they were quick to congratulate him for his placing of the cheese upon the Tucker sandwich.

"We need only get a good night's sleep and wait for the morrow," Pedwyn said, "We can follow the Tucker to make sure he consumes this repast and be on our way." He said this with such conviction the others just simply assumed that is how it would go down. They made a soft nest of pine needles and climbed inside to slumber. Wippa took the first watch, the smell of Tucker feet still in his nose troubled him too much to sleep, but eventually he too fell into unquiet dreams.

<u>18</u>

Tad Tucker was dragging. He was late coming down for breakfast and only had time to grab a piece of bacon before he hurried out the door. He remembered to wish Erin a happy birthday as he gave her a half-way brother kind of hug. His parents had started singing to their daughter as he was coming down the stairs and had given him pestered looks at his missing the beginning of the song. Still, despite his tardiness, his mother was smiling as she handed him his lunch and told him to have a nice day at school. Tad's father echoed this on his own way out the door to work. Tad only half responded to each of them as he got his bike and raced off toward school. He was going to tell Luke about the footprints and try to get his friend to believe him once again, and hopefully come back around to sitting together at lunch. As he thought of lunch his grumbling stomach reminding him that a single piece of bacon was not going to suffice since he had been sent to bed the night before without dinner. Tad slowed down a bit and began to extract the snacks and fruit from his lunch to hungrily consume as he peddled. He would save his sandwich for later. He rapidly scarfed his food as he peddled faster and down the road out of sight of the Faerie troop he had no idea were watching him leave.

BeBoo Pevin recoiled his See-Scope and sighed.

"He's gone around the corner. I can't see him anymore," the Pixie said. "Maybe if we had gotten up earlier like

137

we planned we would have been ready for this," he added smarmily.

"Goodness me!" Pedwyn wailed, "I was up and more than ready. In fact, I woke YOU up!"

"Well, you did not wake us up in time for a good breakfast," the Pixie retorted, "we have a Bogie with us Pedwyn, you can't possibly think he can function without a good breakfast, none of us can."

Hetchy mewled low and sad, and then said something along the lines of "Mufprr." Pedwyn rolled his eyes sharply and wrinkled his brow. He was all prepared to whine about Fee's snoring putting him into such a tranquil sleep he could not possibly wake up in time, but knew his friends would never accept his complaining of the melodic soothing beauty of the Dink's snore. He kept quiet and just gave up, as he gathered their things and covered the signs of their nesting.

"Fine," he said, "there is no use getting rolled up about it. We missed our chance to follow the Tucker and watch him eat the cheese."

"Well, he was going very fast Pedwyn, and your plan was ridiculous," BeBoo said with a snort, reminding Pedwyn how he sillily thought one could use a Star-Hat in the day time!

Their argument was interrupted as Erin Tucker opened the door and bolted from the house. She had a red birthday sash around her chest and carried two balloons with her in joyous celebration of reaching the wizened age of seven. Her mother walked her to the end of the driveway where she met several other children to await the coming of the bus. The parents briefly interacted before returning inside to watch from their windows. The children having long ago made it clear how uncool it was to have their parents wait with them. During all this, the Faeries returned to their crumpled pine nest beneath the bush and observed. Pedwyn turned when he saw the large yellow bus coming down the street, noticed the children began to line up and watch as it approached, and correctly ascertained that this was the system they used to get to school. Having no clear idea how to get them all aboard the large vessel, Pedwyn quickly reacted and turned his attention to the Dink.

"Miss Fee?" he asked, "do you think you can go about this alone? Do you think you can manage?" he asked, completely trusting the Dink to journey to the Tucker's school, find him amongst all the other children, and make sure he ate his sandwich. Fee stood tall, as tall as she could, and simply nodded with confidence. She knew enough to not risk chirping here in the broad daylight. Wippa snorted his skepticism that she would not find the Tucker without his tracking ability, but Pedwyn placed all his confidence in his tiny blue Faery friend.

"Go Miss Fee, Go now!" he said in haste, "And we will wait for you here."

Fee the Dink held her breath and swelled up to twice her normal size, then slowly exhaled and began to shrink. None

139

of the other Faeries had ever witnessed this Dink ability before, but as they watched Fee the Dink dwindled down to the size of a fly. Off she flew towards the children as they boarded the bus. Pedwyn squinted, but Wippa was able to see her enter the vehicle and find a place inside Erin's backpack. He related this to Pedwyn, and the troop sank down into the pine straw. They all knew they had a long wait ahead in hopes their mission would soon end.

"Now," Pedwyn said, and turned to Hetchy as he said it, "let us all eat a proper breakfast."

Meanwhile, Tad Tucker peddled himself up to the bike rack, quickly locked his front tire to the bar, and started toward the side entrance he and Luke normally utilized for stressless non-bully access to class. If Tad Tucker's morning had started off well, it suddenly went sour as he rounded the corner and saw Chuck Bain and his browbeater band lurking by the door. Tad quickly tried to turn back around the wall's edge, but Chuck called out to him before he could vanish.

"Tadpole, the Elf-Boy!" Chuck Bain roared for all to hear. Tad's shoulders sank and he turned back around.

"Shut-up Chuck," he defiantly said back, "you know we will both be suspended if we fight again." They had both been warned by the Principal that any future fighting would result in heavy sanctions, and while this concerned Tad a great deal, Chuck Bain had a reputation to uphold, and suspensions only strengthened the mythic status of the meanest kid in the school.

"You better be careful telling me to shut-up Tucker," Chuck snarled, "Or do I need to remind you that you still have a black eye."

Tad winced at that, while the eye was getting a bit better, and his mother had iced it for him ever since the incident, he had almost forgotten the ugly yellowing bruise. He was suddenly reminded the one who had given it was standing in front of him with a clenching fist. Tad thought quickly, remembering how in prior bullying episodes Chuck Bain had taken great delight in forcing him and Luke to hand over their lunches to him and his buddies. Without much fanfare, Tad simply threw his brown bagged lunch in Chuck's direction.

"Here, OK?" he said feigning total submission, "can we just go to class now please?"

Chuck looked at the brown bag on the ground before him and grinned. He motioned for one of his minions to retrieve it for him and then smiled at all those watching.

"Wise decision Elf-Boy," he crowed, "But don't ever tell me to shut up again." He said this to all listening to let them realize he should and could have wailed on Tad for such an offense, but that brown bag payment would suffice today due to his obvious generosity. Several kids nearby, including Patty Green, simply rolled their eyes. Though, they did so without Chuck or his gang seeing them do it. Tad was half way in the door when he heard Chuck shouting from behind him.

"Hey! There is only a sandwich in here! Where are all the goodies? Tucker, you bum! I'll get you for this!" He continued to storm as Tad sped up and raced down the hall towards class.

The first half of the school day seemed to stretch on forever to Tad. He tried to make eye contact with Luke, but his former best friend was not making it easy. He heard whispers and giggles from behind him in class as Chuck muttered about the morning's events, and the teasing label of "Elf-Boy" was heard more than a few times. Tad suffered through, and eventually found himself in the lunchroom where he was reminded; he was without a meal. He was prepared to sit across from Luke and once again attempt to make peace, but decided to wait and instead get into the line where he would be forced to charge his lunch. He knew his mother would ask later why he owed the school money, and he would have to come up with some white lie about dropping his lunch in a puddle or something. As Tad stood in line, inching closer toward the stack of trays and his eventual meal, he was unaware of being under the observation of a tiny blue fly-sized Faery.

Fee the Dink had extracted herself from Erin's backpack and spent the better part of the day flying unseen throughout the school hallways, peering into every door until she had found the Tucker. She had lit in the corner of his classroom and observed as he and his classmates lined up for their walk down the hallways and into the larger lunchroom. Here she knew her duty was to make sure he ate his Mooncheese-laced sandwich.

Concern crossed her small blue face when she did not see him sitting and eating along with the other human children. As it became clear that the Tucker was in line to obtain food, Fee could only correctly assume something had gone wrong with the plan. Realizing she herself possessed a piece of Mooncheese; she chose to act.

Now, as Fee displayed her shrinking ability earlier to her friends, it should be noted that all possessions of Dinks magically alter along with the dwindling fairies. That one of the smallest species of the Little People should possess the ability to shrink even smaller, was such a shocking and seemingly unimportant capability to those who studied such things, no one was ever really sure how their possessions shrank along with them. The elders and wisest of the Faeries, along with the scribes who recorded all their histories, had never really much cared to record an abundance of Dinklore. Dinks were simply there to amuse their neighbors, providing melodic backdrops to daily events and various party settings. That they possessed their own unique history and powerset was something still to be discovered. Though Fee's shrinking ability had provided her the means to easily follow Erin and find the Tucker, she was now faced with a new problem. Her Mooncheese, in her current state, was simply too small to be effective if she were to successfully put it into the Tucker's meal. She had to risk returning to her normal size. While she would still be quite small, the danger of being noticed was still there.

Tad turned the corner into the final segment of the lunch line. As he smelled the food, he was reminded he had not eaten much other than junk in the last two days. He knew most kids made fun of the school's fare, but he himself actually enjoyed the chicken patty sandwiches and pizza. Today, he would chose the chicken sandwich, and he informed the lunch lady of this as she lazily swatted away a tiny fly. That she had to sway a fly from landing on the food was sadly nothing new to her or to the children about to eat the offerings. That this particular fly was blue, and actually not a fly, was lost to them in this moment.

"Here you go Thaddeus," Mrs. Burles the lunch lady said, taking great delight in using his given name as she thought it was rather Biblical and had a great-Uncle with the same moniker. Tad of course, hated her usage of it in front of the other kids and made a face letting her know this.

"Thanks," he said cynically, and moved on down the line to let the cashier know he would have to charge his meal. She handed him a charge slip and reminded him to have his parents sign in and return it with the money, or to put money into his account. Tad nodded in understanding and was about to move out of the line when he heard Milly Sanders from behind him.

"Is that a Smurf doll?" she asked, rather loudly.

Tad turned back confused as he noticed she was pointing down at his lunch tray. There on his tray next to his chicken sandwich, somehow, was a small one-inch blue figure. He stared down at it and then back at Milly.

"Did you put that there?" he asked questionably. "Did you?" he asked back at Mrs. Burles as Milly was shaking her head. Mrs. Burles looked at him obliviously and went about serving other children their lunch choices.

"You really do have a thing for dolls huh, Tad?" Milly asked.

"That is not my Smurf!" was all Tad could manage, and he realized how utterly silly that sounded. As other kids began to snicker, he grasped he was the butt of someone's joke and grabbed the small stiff figure and tossed it into the nearby trashcan. The kids following behind him whispered "Doll Boy" and "Elf Boy", echoing what Chuck Bain had started. Tad sought the safety of his table with Luke and sat across from his friend as Milly and the others passed by giving him strange looks and whispering.

"Looks like trouble follows you," Luke Monroe said quietly, hanging his head down so the others did not notice him.

"Someone put a Happy Meal toy on my tray, trying to be funny," Tad told Luke, deciding that is what had happened. Luke merely shrugged and gave a look that implied Tad had brought this upon himself. Tad began to deflect, telling Luke why he was forced to charge lunch that day. They both looked over to where Chuck was wolfing down various parts of obtained cuisine.

"Some things will never change," Luke stated.

"Have we changed?" Tad asked. "Are you still mad at me, not wanting to have me sit here?" He started to tell Luke about the footprints in the cake, but Luke stopped him.

"Tad, please, this is getting out of control. I just really don't want to hear any more about this Elf stuff, OK?" he said. Tad started to rebut, but sadly looked down and realized all the excitement he felt about revealing new details really were not going to prove anything. His best friend did not believe him. No one believed him. His mood began to sour, and he sat quietly listening to the raucous murmurs of his fellow classmates, who enjoyed their lunchtime gatherings the way inmates must enjoy yard time.

Meanwhile, from the depths of the bitter-smelling lunch room trashcan of Southern Shores Middle School, a small "Smurf" extracted herself. Fee the Dink held her breath for two reasons. The stench of the human waste-filled bucket was assaulting her nostrils, and she needed to utilize her shrinking ability once again. As she held her breath and swelled to twice her normal size, she began to rapidly decrease in volume until she was once again small enough to fly undetected out of the garbage can and up to the highest point of where the wall met the ceiling to alight and observe. From her perch, Fee could see the entirety of the lunch room and look down upon Tad and his

146

friend. She was rather proud of herself for what had just transpired. She had flown down on Tad's lunch tray, lit beneath his foil-covered sandwich, and crawled inside the opening. Once inside the foil wrapping, she had released her breath and grown to her full, but still tiny, size. At that point, she had placed her piece of Mooncheese beneath the bread and upon the circular meat patty of the Tucker's lunch. Here she made her mistake, for as she exited the foil, she was suddenly aware of the extremely unfamiliar sense of human eyes upon her. Fee's first instinct was to stiffen. This is apparently another special power of the Dinks, and it is obvious Hollow Hill scholars are way behind on chronicling all the skills of these small creatures. Anyway, as she became rigid, the human children had thankfully mistaken her for a toy. While the Shee-Queen's warning of trusting to their species ability to not be seen was ardent and strict, her particular abilities allowed her to be witnessed, though theoretically, not noticed. Fee the Dink had therefore not actually violated the Shee-Queen's warning. She was however, at this point, really getting impatient with Tad Tucker.

Tad sat quietly across from Luke and finally found the courage to speak as he noticed the waning moments of their lunchtime break evident on the large clock attached to the wall.

"Luke are you sure you don't want to hear..." he was about to ask more.

"Are you going to eat that?" Luke asked, pointing towards Tad's chicken, indicating that while his friend had casually eaten a few of his crinkle fries, he had left the sandwich untouched.

"What?" Tad said confused, "Oh, um, no you can have it, I guess I lost my appetite."

"Don't forget to study for the tests we have coming up," Luke said, knowing his friend would think he was a broken record on that subject and preparing himself for Tad to say something negative back to him.

"Yeah," Tad said slowly, "yeah sure." With that he slid off his seat, carried his tray back to the return, and slowly walked back to class as Luke watched him go. The other kids finished their lunches and filed out in their own fashion as a small blue fly-sized Faery finally let loose a long low sad frustrated whistle and flew out the slightly open window.

19

As Tad Tucker retrieved his bicycle from the rack, he spotted Chuck Bain's crony gang standing nearby and thought to himself how it could be possible they were always here before he could sneak away. However, Chuck was not yet present, and his band seemed immobilized without their intimidating leader. While they awaited his arrival, Tad was thankful for the reprieve and utilized this narrow window to escape the confounds of Southern Shores Middle School. As he peddled away, he reflected on his day, and the days prior, and to all the escalating consequences of seeing his Elf. He thought of how his best friend no longer wanted to hang out with him, how his enemies were having a field day at his expense, how his temper had landed him in the Principal's office, how bad his grades were recently, and how upset his parents were with him. In the back of his mind he began to ask himself if he might be a little crazy after all. Maybe, it was all a coincidence, and a doll shoe was there with swamp muck causing it to smell, and it was raining extremely hard when he thought he saw this creature; so possibly it was all in his head. He could not believe he was now trying to convince himself it was all untrue. If this is how he felt, then what had been the point of all this? This was the first time, but it was not going to be the last time, where he allowed himself to doubt what he had so fiercely believed since that rainstorm sighting from his parent's station wagon window. Maybe he had been wrong all along? And if that were true, the trouble it was causing was not worth it. Tad thought maybe he was better off never thinking about, or bringing up, his Elf sighting ever again. Emotions welled up inside him as he fought back tears. All of this began to swirl around his head until he found himself aimlessly circling his bicycle back around toward the school. He was subconsciously avoiding going home even though he knew the family had dinner plans later for Erin's birthday. Remembering his sister's birthday made him think of the yelling at the table, her cake, and the footprints he swore were there on the icing. His parents did not believe him, and now he was wondering if even the footprints were a trick of his mind. But they had looked so convincingly real. How had his family not seen it too? Just when he had begun to wonder if he were becoming delusional, his recollection of the perfectly formed footprints on the cake made him even more confused. Though, it was all still possible he was seeing what he wanted to see.

Tad Tucker parked his bike and sat on a bench in a playground near his neighborhood. He sat there thinking thoughts a ten-year-old boy should never have to imagine. He remembered his parents whispering something about his dad's oldest aunt "acting crazy", and having something called "early on set", or something else he was not sure about. He worried now that he too was going crazy, how he was seeing things that were not there, a little man in the mist, footprints on a cake. His emotions again began to well up inside of him and he sat there holding back more tears. Tad Tucker had so wanted this day to be a good day, to be different from how he was currently feeling, but all of it caught up to him and he began to softly sob alone on the park bench.

"Tad?" he heard a soft female voice ask out, "are you crying?"

Tad looked up to see his worst nightmare standing before him. Patty Greene was there along with the Dowdy girls, who were giggling silently behind her as they all stopped to witness his breakdown. He had been so lost in his worries he failed to hear them approaching. He quickly wiped his eyes and denied her accusation.

"No!" he said firmly, "of course not." Tad tried to look away, pretending he was unconcerned with them standing there, but inside he was hoping they would just leave. He was now losing count of how many times this week Patty Greene had seen him in an embarrassing position.

"Are you sure you're OK, Tad?" Patty asked again, trying to actually sound concerned. "Where is Luke? I heard you two weren't talking anymore. Is that true?" Patty motioned for the snickering Dowdy girls to go on without her, telling them she would catch up soon. She turned back to Tad, but he was already standing up and getting onto his bicycle.

"Luke isn't here now, is he? So why don't you catch up to your big-mouthed friends and leave me alone!" Tad yelled, surprising both himself and Patty with his emotional outburst.

"What has gotten into you lately Tad?" Patty queried, "We used to actually be friends you know?"

"You were never my friend! You have been laughing along with all the others this whole year. Laughing at me and Luke getting teased and picked on. Laughing this whole week at my...story," he trailed off, not wanting to talk about his Elf anymore.

"That's not fair Tad! Everyone was laughing at those things!" Patty yelled back.

"Patty just go please! Take your gossipy friends and leave me alone!" Tad yelled back too. He realized he had never yelled at Patty before, and had never heard her raise her voice to him. Patty looked surprised, shocked, and a little upset, as she spun and ran toward her friends. When she reached them, she looked back at Tad with sadness in her eyes and it haunted him the rest of that day. He had grown up a few streets over from Patty Greene and they had known each other since pre-school. He would never have admitted this to any of his friends, but he tended to sit up straight and be on his best behavior whenever Patty was nearby. This trend had been tested during this tumultuous last few days and Tad Tucker was grimly aware that his feelings for Patty Greene were strangely unfamiliar to a ten-year-old boy. The trials and tribulations of a fourth-grade crush can never be explained but should never be underestimated. As he watched her walk away, he once again began to regret this whole affair. Tad Tucker may have been far removed from any ability to recognize the first pangs of the emotion called love, however; Fee the Dink was drawn to it like a moth to a shining light.

In Hollow Hill, the Dink tribe tend to overlook boundary fences. Though most troop-type Fae unite into colonies of locality, the Dinks flit about Faerie where they please. They establish short-lived villages from time to time, but mostly just move in migratory patterns wherever the prettiest flowers are currently in bloom. As previously pointed out, there have been no official studies published on the history and traits of this particular Faerie type, and most just assume the Dinks are clever enough to hang out in areas of well-mannered folk and pretty things. For example, no Dink has ever been sighted near Creech Hill, nor the Shallow Moors, or any of the darker less-friendly places. But were one to really start to track such things, they would realize the Dinks are being drawn to emotions of love and tenderness. Most everyone assumes they like the flowers and pretty hills, and honestly, they do, but what draws them to these places, like a primal instinctual pull, are the emotional responses emitted by others in the vicinity. Flowers tend to elicit smiles and good feelings, so too the soft grass-covered vales of Hollow Hill, thus; the Dinks flock to these locations like small blue bees to honey.

Patty Greene may not have realized she was wanting to be tender and kind to Tad Tucker after she noticed his distress, and Tad Tucker had no idea he was experiencing any warm feelings toward her, but Fee the Dink picked up on them both and easily relocated the Tucker, whom she had previously lost in the confusing stampede of children following the final school bell ringing. Still in her small fly-sized form, she hovered overhead and witnessed the entire final exchange between the two, her head slightly stinging at the emotional outburst and change in them both. Still, she could sense the deeper emotions hidden within each of them. However, those emotions would have to wait for another time. Tad furiously peddled back home, and Fee flew high above, using him as her guide back to the house of the Tucker.

Once they arrived back at the residence, Tad parked his bicycle in the garage and raced inside. Fee the Dink flew down beneath the bush, returned to her full size, and began to search for her friends. Wippa emerged from the shrubbery and nodded toward the Dink. Fee could tell he was glad to see her safely returned, though if asked, Wippa would deny ever expressing the slightest concern. But both of them knew, the only time he ever smiled, which was a grim looking thing on a Spriggan face, was when he and Fee were alone and no one else would notice. She flew up to him and allowed him to briefly pat her curly-cued blue bulb head before he quickly pulled away and feigned disinterest. Fee cooed questionably as to the others and Wippa pointed lazily toward the underbrush. There she saw the other three curled up in a lazy napping knot within a hastily made nest. Wippa had arranged enough leaves and pine straw around them to hide them from sight, and was undoubtably foregoing his own nap time in order to stand guard. Fee turned back smiling and cheeped at Wippa in her own way of expressing gratitude for his being their guardian and protector, but the Spriggan just turned away pretending not to care. Fee smiled wider and turned toward her sleeping companions. She gave a sharp tonal whistle, and they all three jumped awake.

"Goodness me!" Pedwyn Dale shrieked, which was half muffled by his beard being in his mouth. "Fee, you are back! Wonderful! Wonderful! Did the Tucker eat the Mooncheese? Can we all go home now? Do you think the Shee-Queen's magic will just retrieve us from here or do we have to journey back over that darned ditch again? Thank you so much for assisting on this Miss Fee, it has really been...."

"Pedwyn will you be quiet!" BeBoo Pevin harshly grumbled, "Look at her face. Have you ever seen her NOT smiling?" The Pixie pointed at the Dink's sullen expression. Pedwyn noticed it instantly and stopped his thankful speech.

"Miss Fee?" he asked softly, "did our plan go as intended?"

Fee the Dink lowered her head and tried to force a frown. Dinks lack the facial muscle structure to frown, so it came across as if she misunderstood the question. Pedwyn repeated himself.

"Did the Tucker eat the Mooncheese BeBoo placed upon his sandwich?" he asked again with waning hope, "Please tell us that you witnessed the Tucker eat the sandwich, Fee."

155

Fee the Dink shook her teardrop-shaped head from side to side and all the gathered Faerie's shoulders slumped together in frustration.

"Tell us what happened Miss Fee," Pedwyn asked sullenly, the dream of soon returning to his untidy house back in Hollow Hill was fading faster than he hoped it would.

One must be careful when asking a Dink to tell a story. They are more than capable of answering simple yes or no questions with a chirp or a beep. And most Fae are equally capable of interpreting a Dink's response. But having a Dink relate an entire tale is a risky venture. The melodic musically fluid language of these small blue Faeries tends to put the listener into a tranquil repose which eventually leads to a deep slumber before the tale is even remotely close to being finished. Once on the anniversary of their most endearing holiday, Darby the Dink told a tale involving the entirety of the Dink lineage. When his narrative was complete everyone in attendance was already fast asleep and dozed through until the day after the holiday, missing the entire point.

Fee began to relate her story, starting from Erin's backpack and going forward. Pedwyn had to be jostled awake at the point where she put her own slice of Mooncheese onto the sandwich, completely slept through the part of her stiffening, and then woke up again at the end with her watching the boy and the girl exchange yells.

"So, to be clear," he reiterated, "the Tucker did not eat either slice?"

"No Pedwyn!" BeBoo retorted, "were you not listening?" BeBoo then gave a quicker recap of Fee's epic saga, and Pedwyn came to accept that they needed yet another plan. He started to throw ideas out to the others on how they could finally get the Tucker to eat the Mooncheese. Wippa decided he had heard enough.

The Spriggan had managed to stay awake during the entirety of Fee's telling, with the part about the lunch room line most intriguing him. He thought to ask her to explain it again, but rather than risk falling asleep at her melodic musings, he determined he would have to see for himself. Spriggans, for their part, are as crafty and strategic as any species in Faerie. They have gotten themselves into so much mischief throughout their history that forming plans to avoid trouble, or solve problems, is naturally woven into their genetic makeup. Wippa had played thoughts and plans around in his mind ever since Fee's return. His first idea was to slink back into the kitchen, place his slice of Mooncheese on the Tucker sandwich, then go to Chuck Bain's house and bite him so hard he would be unable to attend school the following day. This would make it impossible for him to steal the Tucker's lunch. While that would be the most entertaining venture for him, he wisely decided it would also be the most precarious. From what Fee had earlier related, he concluded that while it was easy to sneak the cheese onto the boy's meal at night, it was too unpredictable to know if that lunch would make it inside the school. He also thought how he could creep into the human kitchen and tear the bottom of the Tucker's lunch bag. This would allow the contents to eventually spill out, forcing him into this lunch line the Dink described. From there, he imagined how he could easily sneak the cheese onto the school meal. Attempting to predict all the eventual outcomes led the Spriggan to one simple conclusion. No matter if the Tucker brought his own lunch or was forced to get one from the school, his slice of Mooncheese would end up on that sandwich. He would already be there to make sure.

Wippa related his plan to the group of Fae friends and despite some muttering objections from each of them, they all agreed that the skill of the Spriggan was best suited to carry out this endeavor. They just collectively dreaded spending another day beneath that bush.

The Faerie band hunkered beneath the front yard hedges of the Tucker family and waited. They observed the family leaving for Erin's celebration and realized they then had free reign within the residence. Having lingered until dusk, they crept back into the ventilation system and once again into the Tucker kitchen. This was a first time for most of them, and they delighted in exploring the strange surroundings, though BeBoo lamented being told to stay completely away from the cake. Wippa had decided to check to see if the Tucker lunch had been prepared by the mother, and had reluctantly allowed his companions to join him. He saw there was no ready meal and realized his options were now limited. While they were in the house, he decided to re-check a previous failure.

Wippa scurried across the kitchen floor to the bottom of the carpet-covered stairwell. Pedwyn was busying himself directing everyone to not touch anything and leave every item as they found it when he noticed the Spriggan ascend the stairs.

"Where is he going?" BeBoo Pevin inquired.

"I suspect I know," Pedwyn replied, "and unless I miss my guess he will be back down soon." Pedwyn realized the Spriggan was going to check once more to see if the boy's bedroom provided an opportunity to just simply wait until he fell asleep and cram the Mooncheese into his mouth. But the last time they tried this they were thwarted by something even the Spriggan could not successfully maneuver around. Wippa's quick return downstairs signaled to Pedwyn and the others that the boy had yet to clean his room, and a dirty sock was still present on the floor beneath the bed.

"Still there?" Pedwyn asked expectedly. The Spriggan scrunched his nose and hissed, giving them all every indication the sock was indeed still there. They all shook their heads unable to believe the horrendous habits of human children.

Wippa's plan was now down to one solution. He would carry his slice of Mooncheese into the school building himself. He would wait there patiently to put it on whatever the child ate the following day. This seemed like an impossible risk to most, but Pedwyn and the others realized the only one of them possessing the means to carry it through was their Spriggan ally.

They all returned outside the house to their makeshift nest where Wippa actually took the time to touch them all and take whatever luck they had to offer before he made his way through the neighborhood to the Tucker school.

"Heed the Shee-Queen's wisdom my friend. May you enter and exit on your own terms," Pedwyn Dale said, trying to sound filled with wisdom and leadership. Wippa frowned and simply nodded. He looked at Fee in a way which told her she was to watch over them while he was gone. She chirped softly and flew around his head until he politely swatted her away.

Double checking to make sure his Mooncheese was still present within its leafy wrappings, he turned to leave his friends. The scent of the Tucker's recent bike ride was all he needed to retrace the journey. When the human children arrived the following day at their place of learning, the Spriggan would already be in place, waiting.

"Will he be OK, Pedwyn?" BeBoo asked, with genuine concern.

"Wippa can take care of himself my little friend. He has proven that time and time again in my dealings with him both back home and here in the World. I suspect he will be successful in his pursuit, and we can look forward to returning home in no time." As he said this, he hoped deep inside he was telling the Pixie the truth. He considered himself the leader of this mission to the World, and it was not in good form to keep sending his fellow Fae out on solo assignments. He was not entirely sure how the Spriggan would be able to keep from being seen and get the cheese into the boy's mouth, but he was so weary of their failures to do so at this juncture that he was willing to just pin all his hopes on the most disreputable of their pack.

"The Spriggan will do just fine," he said aloud, trying to convince himself as well as the others, "just fine indeed."

"I hope so," BeBoo responded.

20

Erin's birthday party had gone well, and Tad Tucker had for a small amount of time forgotten his troubles. Despite the annoying squeals of several girls his younger sister's age dancing around the restaurant while chasing a teenager in an oversized mouse costume, Tad still managed to enjoy himself. Their parents had not fought, and actually seemed to get along. Perhaps they were putting aside their own troubles long enough to let their daughter enjoy her special day. Tad stayed quiet in the back of the station wagon as one by one Erin's friends were dropped off and the family returned into their driveway. He exited the vehicle and raced inside, wanting to just go upstairs and finally be alone. He yelled back at his parents that he had homework, but they were so overly focused on Erin and bringing all her presents inside, they simply waved their son on.

The next morning Tad woke up late and ran downstairs for a quick breakfast. He was surprised to see his father and mother still in their pajamas and his lunch not yet prepared.

"Mom!" he said loudly, "I'm going to be late. Why didn't you yell for me to come down?" He grabbed a banana and a juice box and began to head out the door. "And you forgot to pack my lunch. Did you both oversleep too?" he asked.

"Seems so," his father said quickly, and went back to reading his paper, "hopefully the world won't grind to a halt if your mother and I take a Friday off from work," he joked. "But it just might if you are late for school, so get going, Tiger!"

"But my lunch?!" Tad said again loudly.

"Oh here, just buy your lunch today, OK?" his mother said, handing him money. Tad realized it was more than enough to buy a lunch and to secretly pay for the one he was forced to buy yesterday. He waited for his mother to demand her change, but she did not, and he kept quiet.

Tad opened the door leading to the garage and toward his bike. He looked back in expectation of some scolding reminder about bringing up his grades or not fighting at school, but his parents seemed overly distracted in an almost annoying way.

"Where's Erin?" he asked back into the kitchen.

"She was picked up this morning by Gilly's mom," his mother answered, "they are going to buy her a birthday breakfast treat and drop her off at school."

"How long is she going to milk this birthday thing?" Tad asked incredulously.

"Thaddeus," his mother smiled, "go to school!"

"Fine," he said, and closed the door.

When he arrived at school there were only a few stragglers outside. He was running so late he lacked the time to try the side entrance in order to avoid Chuck and his friends. Thankfully, they were not around, and he assumed they were probably already in the classroom. He quickly locked his bicycle and raced to class seconds before the opening bell sounded.

As Tad entered the classroom, he was surprised to notice so few children sitting at their desks. He scanned the room quickly and noticed half the classroom was missing. These absent students included most of the ones he sat near, and thankfully Chuck Bain and most of his rabble. He looked confused toward Mrs. Littlefield.

"Glad you could make it today, Tad," she teased, even though he had technically made it inside the room just as the bell was ringing. "Let's see," she continued, "Tucker. There you are. You are staying here with me this morning. Have a seat, please." Tad sat down even more puzzled.

"But I'm here with you every day," he stated, "what is going on?"

"Tad, you have not been doing a very good job of paying attention this week have you?" Mrs. Littlefield stated correctly, having no idea how correct she really was, "Half the class is going to the computer lab today for testing. Since they do not have enough seats in there for everyone we have to go in shifts, do you remember we talked about this? We do this every Friday now Tad. You will get to go after lunch."

165

He did not remember having talked about this at all, but as he scanned the room, he realized that not only were Chuck and most of his posse gone, but so too were Luke, Patty, and both Dowdy sisters. He closed his eyes briefly and thanked his luck for small miracles.

His day easily raced by, though with such a small classroom he was called upon to answer more than he would normally have liked, and was forced to actually pay close attention to the lesson plan. As midday neared the students returned from the computer lab in order to rejoin their classroom for lunch. Tad saw Chuck holding the door open for everyone and waited for him to slam it in someone's face, but he never did. Tad suspected Chuck probably knew Mrs. Littlefield was watching for just such a move. As the room refilled, Tad avoided the eyes of most of his classmates, looking down as if he were deeply into the open book before him. Eventually, the lunch bell rang, and Tad hurried towards the cafeteria. Bringing one's lunch allowed for a more leisurely pace, but when one had to buy a lunch, it was first come first serve total chaos.

Tad grabbed a lunch tray, and lined up within the queue. To his chagrin Patty Greene ended up behind him, and the Dowdy girls were right behind her. So much for small miracles, he thought. Tad slid closer toward the food, keeping his eyes forward and down, while ignoring the whispers from behind him. He scanned the day's fare which consisted of the fish sandwiches he generally found disgusting, and thankfully a limited amount of pizza that he hoped would still be there when his turn came. However, true to Tad Tucker's current luck streak, Lester Leggett was in front of him in line. Lester was not only the fattest kid in his grade, but also had a set of parents who catered to his every whim. Tad knew what was about to happen and was not let down when Lester Leggett asked Mrs. Burles for three slices of pizza.

"Dang Lester!" he said audibly.

"What?" the heavyset boy exclaimed, "it's a free country."

Tad scowled at him as he moved his tray down the line with a smirky look on his round face. "That doesn't even make sense in this situation," Tad said back.

"Don't bitch so much Tad, I left you a piece anyway," Lester shouted back as he turned the corner to pay for his meal, all three of them.

"Did you hear that?" Tad asked Mrs. Burles suggestively.

"Not my concern," she retorted, 'what will it be today Thadd...um..Tad," she remembered to not embarrass him. As she asked, she shifted her hair within the net that kept it in place. This network of string kept her locks in a taut bun and stretched tightly across her forehead giving her a humorous look that most children were so used to at this point they no longer laughed at the sight. However, the look she projected did momentarily distract the Spriggan.

Wippa had entered the school easily the night before, explored its vast surroundings a bit, then wisely found a dark hiding place and caught up on much needed sleep. Bells stirred him in the morning, and he consumed a quick breakfast he had foraged on the way across town. He used the vent system to find his way into the cafeteria and from there was able to look down as the human kitchen staff cleaned and prepared. He took amusement in observing the human activity and daydreamed several times of pinching, poking, or setting small fires in the kitchen to occupy his boredom. Eventually, he made his way out of the vent and slinked down to the exact spot he needed to be to correctly surmise the Tucker's desire for that last piece of something called pizza. As Mrs. Burles asked Tad for the second time what he wanted to eat, and as he was in the motion of pointing toward that last offering, Wippa's lanky arm shot out and placed his Mooncheese upon the pizza slice, retracting his limb with such blinding speed no one could have ever noticed. Before she even finished her sentence, he was back up the wall and into the vent looking down on his achievement. As Mrs. Burles placed the choice upon Tad's tray, Wippa smiled to himself in wicked glee how he would be able to report back to the others the resounding success of his task. He thought of how happy the Shee-Queen would be with him for having been the one to accomplish it. He turned to venture around the vent system in order to look down into the lunch room to actually observe the boy digest the meal, when a delicate female voice stopped him in his tracks.

"Was that the last piece of pizza, Mrs. Burles?" Patty Greene asked, in such a sweet sounding voice it even briefly made the Spriggan stop. Its effect on Tad Tucker was much more profound.

"I'm afraid it was, Patty. We had an incident with the dough turning bad this morning and we could only save a small amount. So, we had to resort to thawing out the fish sandwiches that were on Monday's menu." Hearing this caused Wippa to smack his head on his hand, because while he had mainly behaved himself in the Spriggan sense, it was eventually more than he could take, and he had crept down and peed in the pizza dough when the human backs were turned. He realized this was about to backfire on him as he heard the Tucker respond.

"Here Patty," he said gallantly, "you can have my slice."

"Are you sure, Tad?", I mean..." she trailed off obviously hinting at their recent encounter and him having no reason to be overly nice to her.

"No, no, take it, I really like the fish sandwiches here," he lied.

"Thank you, Tad, that's so sweet," she said kindly.

In that moment, none of the children, or the lunch workers, heard a small retching sound coming from the vent system. Wippa did not even linger to watch the results. He knew

169

he had failed. His journey back to his companions was long and slow.

21

Tad Tucker rolled out of bed on this Saturday morning, reluctantly accepting he had to somehow muster the energy to go play a soccer game. He quietly ate breakfast with the family while his parents chatted on with Erin, discussed errands they had to run later that day, and also playfully teased him about his black eye. Which by that point had turned into a yellow-green kaleidoscope of fading painful memory.

"Are you going to be able to play goalie with that swollen eye, Tad?" his father queried, half-jokingly, half concerned.

"Yes," he responded, "I'll be fine."

"Good to know, I'll go get dressed and we can head out, it's just you and me today, Tiger. Your mom is taking Erin to spend some of her birthday money."

"Still with the birthday? Oh my God!" Tad complained, "What, is it the entire month?"

"Thaddeus!" his mother yelled softly, "what's the big deal if your sister has a nice long birthday week? How does that affect you any, Mister?"

"I guess it doesn't, but whatever," he trailed off. Erin stuck her tongue out at him from behind her mother's back. Tad returned the gesture, but with his middle finger.

"Mom!" Erin yelled, "he shot me the bird!"

"Thaddeus!" Helen Tucker shrieked, attempting to sound motherly, "you apologize this instant."

"Oh, let him be a boy, and an annoying big brother," his father said playfully from behind his wife, while at the same time rolling up the newspaper and smacking her on the behind. "Ooh!" his wife shrieked, while jumping away. "Ronald!" she said laughing.

Tad watched this lighthearted exchange in confusion. He shook his head at Erin, who simply shrugged her shoulders at him, then defiantly shot him a little bird of her own.

"I'm going to put my cleats on," Tad said loudly to escape the insanity of his family kitchen.

While Tad was in the garage locating his footwear, Wippa slunk back down from the ventilation system where he had been eavesdropping, and returned to the hidden campsite of his companions. They had relocated their hideaway from beneath the front yard hedge to the relative safety of a small landscaped wood line in the back corner of the property.

"Did you pick up any clues my Spriggan friend?" Pedwyn Dale inquired hopefully.

Wippa began to make guttural shifting sentences in the Spriggan tongue so quickly that Pedwyn had to slow him down in order to interpret for the others. Wippa recanted what he had overheard while Pedwyn turned to the others and translated.

"They have no big yellow carriage coming today, it is a day of recreation, the Tucker mother angered him, and he said he would Sock Her, then he shot a bird and the father hit his mother with a rolled up weapon and she cried. Then the sister also shot a bird. There, that is about it," Pedwyn Dale incorrectly related, "Oh, and the Tucker is going to play a game called Cleats."

"What do they have against birds?" BeBoo Pevin asked angrily.

"I am not sure, but we best keep Fee from flying by their windows. I think this situation is getting worse by the day," Pedwyn declared, exasperated. With that, the Faeries hunkered down and began to go over plans one by one as to how they could finally get the Tucker to eat a piece of Mooncheese so they could return home. Pedwyn asked them all to relax, take in the beauty of their small wood-like surroundings, let it remind them of home, and try to come up with the best idea possible.

"We do not dare try to follow the Tucker at this point," Pedwyn said, "but we can wait here until he returns. By then, I am positive I will have come up with a fantastic plan. But if any of you have a thought, please feel free to offer it up, and I will put it under consideration."

BeBoo looked at Wippa and they both rolled their eyes. They knew Pedwyn was fresh out of ideas, and they would have to put their heads together to think of one.

Tad Tucker stared out the window of the station wagon and ignored his father who was singing along to the radio and sporadically trying to inspire him to play a good game. He had to give his dad credit for keeping up appearances, but he knew things were not going well with his parents relationship. He also knew his dad was still upset with him for the fights, and the bad grades, but apparently today he was going to let things go, at least until after the game. Tad normally enjoyed alone time with his father, and also the ability to sit in the front seat, but he was in such a down mood over recent events he could not gather any excitement for conversation with his parent, or for his upcoming match.

Tad went through expected motions during the game, but his mind was not on it, and he unfortunately allowed enough goals for his team to finish on the losing side once again. He was not playing against Chuck Bain's team that day, but he noticed them all bunched along the sideline awaiting the field for their game to follow. He avoided the gaze of Chuck as he gathered his gear. Tad was trying to keep an eye on where the other team was warming up as his coach handed out juice boxes and orange slices, and provided the team with a much-needed pep talk. His dad was waiting for him at the car and there was no way to get there without walking past Chuck Bain. Reluctantly, he lowered his head and tried to just maneuver around them all, but he was clearly noticed.

"You win today, Tucker?" Chuck asked.

"No, we didn't win today," Tad said stoically, assuming Chuck knew that already and was trying to embarrass him.

"Oh well, you'll get 'em next time," he said, as he jogged past and continued to warm up. Tad turned and gave him a look wondering what that statement was supposed to mean. Undoubtedly, he meant that in some mean way, but Tad could not figure out how just yet. Whatever, he thought, it did not matter. He turned away from Chuck Bain, from the soccer field, and from the stares of the other children who were watching them wondering if a third fight was going to break out. He headed toward his father and the safety of the blue station wagon.

On the ride back home, they passed by Wheeler's Pond. Tad glanced out the window toward the same spot he first saw what he thought he saw. He remembered returning there soon after and finding the shoe, and yet somehow getting upset and throwing it away the very next day. What was he thinking? He decided in that moment he would return to this place tomorrow, alone without Luke, to see if he could relocate the shoe he tossed, just to be sure.

Tad and his father returned home before his mother and Erin. He was relieved to have the upstairs bathroom to himself without his sisters interruptions. He took a long shower to wash off the dirt from the game and collect his thoughts. He got dressed, headed back downstairs, made himself a late lunch, and sat down with his father to watch television.

"Luke called while you were in the shower," his Dad said, which surprised Tad to hear.

"He did?" Tad said surprisingly, "I wonder what he wanted?"

"Said to call him back if you wanted to go bike riding," his dad answered, "I told him you just got back from the game, but I'd relay the message."

"He wanted to go bike riding?" Tad asked again.

"That's what he said," his Dad repeated, "isn't that what you boys do?"

"Yeah, it's just...been awhile," Tad said slowly.

"Anyway," his father continued, "if you decide to stay here, I was planning on taking us all out for ice-cream when your mom and Erin get back. My treat!" His father always used that joke.

"OK," Tad said, "that sounds fun dad. I'll stay here. I'll just call Luke back later." He trailed off, unsure if he would or not.

22

The weary Faeries watched the Tucker family all load into their long blue carriage and once again leave the driveway and speed off down the street. They had lain in their small woodsy hiding spot for the better part of the day, though Pedwyn had allowed them to gingerly stretch and explore their surroundings one by one to hopefully inspire them to come up with a new idea.

"Do you think he's moved the sock yet?" BeBoo asked for the seventh time.

"Goodness me Pevin!" Pedwyn said frustratingly, "I am rather sure that sock will remain in its place. That avenue of hope is lost to us. We cannot simply stuff it into his mouth while he sleeps. We have had no luck placing it upon his food either. There has to be a better way."

"What if we liquidized it and somehow got it into his drink? Would it work then?" BeBoo asked, trying to sincerely help, as even he was beginning to get a little homesick. Though, he would have never admitted this to any of them.

"Honestly, I am not sure," Pedwyn answered, "I am no expert on the qualities and properties of Mooncheese. Do any of you know?"

Fee let out a very short succinct chip which indicated she did not know and was weary of thinking, also she missed flowers, and honey. Wippa shrugged his shoulders and kept picking at the ground. The Spriggan seemed more irritable then usual ever since missing out on his opportunity to solve this riddle and impress the Shee-Queen. Pedwyn began to realize he was losing the heart of his companions. Their spirts were being broken by their failures to get the Tucker to forget ever seeing him, and he began to feel responsible, since he was the one who had been seen in the first place. He started to realize the longer his friends tarried in the World, away from the spirit-lifting fields of Faerie, the longer he risked doing them permanent harm in some way.

"What if we did not try to hide?" he said out loud, mostly to himself, but the others picked up on it.

"What do you mean Pedwyn" BeBoo asked. "What do you mean try not to hide?"

"What if we just entered into his room, waited for him to wake up in the morning and get out of bed, then just tackled him to the ground and forced the cheese into his mouth and down his throat" Pedwyn said in haste, seemingly acting out this endeavor as he talked. Fee the Dink sat up. Wippa's eyebrows raised. BeBoo Pevin recoiled a bit and snorted.

"I don't know, Pedwyn," he said, "that sounds so very...physical. Besides, we would all be seen if we did it that way."

"Yes, yes, we would," Pedwyn agreed, 'but that is what I meant by no longer trying to hide."

"I'm not following you," BeBoo said frustrated, "the Shee-Queen told us to stay hidden, blah blah our species, blah blah."

"Did you just blah blah the Shee-Queen?" Pedwyn said aghast.

"Do not change the subject! This is a bad idea!" BeBoo shouted, "the Tucker would see us as we did this, she said to NOT be seen, can you not see the disconnection here?"

"Yes," Pedwyn said rather calmly, "but...would the Tucker not forget he saw us upon digesting the Mooncheese? Where of course we would have already hastily left, with our problems solved."

"Can I remind you, Pedwyn," BeBoo said smartly, "that this is actually YOUR problem."

"Oh, is that how this is going to be now?" Pedwyn said disappointedly, but realizing his fears were coming true, his companions attitudes and hopes were changing, "But you missed my point BeBoo. He would forget us, right?"

"I suppose that is sound logic," BeBoo said, not believing he was seeing Pedwyn's point in all this. He then offered to just use the Glee-Wand and levitate the Mooncheese into the boy's sleeping mouth. Or he could levitate over him with the Star-Hat and drop it down in there. All good ideas he thought.

"Could you do either of those things knowing that sock was there?" Pedwyn asked, actually thinking those ideas might work but presuming the Pixie had forgotten the reason they could not just jump up on the bed in the first place.

"Drat!" I think just knowing that nasty child left a sock under his bed would break my concentration. You are right, Pedwyn," BeBoo said despairingly, "We are back to having to do it your way," he added, "but can we tackle him to the floor if we know the sock is there under the bed? What if while we are there wrestling with him, we actually see it? Ugh! Can you imagine?"

"Honestly, no I cannot," Pedwyn agreed, "I would rather not risk having to see that, or smell that." He fumbled for his piece of Mooncheese as he mumbled, "Maybe we can actually liquefy it. Wait. Where is? Oh, yes, I gave my slice to you for the family meal that first night. We will try to liquify your piece."

"I don't have my piece, Pedwyn," BeBoo said accurately, "I wisely put mine on the Tucker's sandwich that first night too. How was I supposed to know he would throw it at the brute-boy?"

"Well, who still has their piece left?" Pedwyn asked. They both looked to Fee the Dink and remembered her story of sneaking her slice onto the school lunch sandwich which Tad did not eat. They turned to Wippa who showed them his empty leaf wrapping and they both recalled at once how he had used his slice on the pizza lunch the boy had cavalierly given to the girl.

"That means...," Pedwyn trailed off. They all turned around as one.

The Bogie sat still while pondering the skyline. He looked down the surrounding fence line, and out past the varied homes in the Tucker neighborhood. He seemed to be noticing it all for the first time. To their horror they spotted a green leafy wrapping lying empty and discarded at the feet of their rapacious friend.

"Hetchy?" Pedwyn said, his voice shaking with a sinking realization and fear.

As he turned around, there in the combination of the street light glow and the rising moon beams, they noticed the sparkly little blue-green crumbs nestled in the whiskers of Hetchy the Bogie.

"Oh No!" BeBoo whispered.

The Bogie considered them with a concentration they had not seen from him at any point prior to now. He tilted his head slightly to the left and simply said, "Ummm, who are you guys again?"

23

Not that it is proper to admit to such things, but Tad Tucker daydreamed all throughout the church sermon and did not pay attention to anything his Pastor was preaching. This is sadly typical of most ten-year old children, and Tad was no exception on this particular Sunday. His mind was completely preoccupied on Elves, smelly little shoes, footprints, Patty Greene, and the complete mess he had made of everything in one seemingly long week. After church he planned to bike once more to Wheeler's Pond, to the very same spot he first saw what he thought he saw, and also to the direction he remembered flinging that shoe. He thought to call Luke back, but decided it would be best to go alone without any more skepticism from his former best friend.

Before he could head out his mother stopped him.

"Tad," she said quietly, "I know this has been a crazy week, with Erin's birthday, and well, some issues your father and I were dealing with. We have not properly talked with you about these fights, or your grades. Your father and I have been...distracted," she trailed off, "I think it would be good if we all sat down later and discussed some things."

"Mom, please do not ground me right now. You can ground me later, but please let me go now to ride my bike. There is something I have to do, please," Tad Tucker pleaded.

"Do you think you should be grounded, Tad?" his mother asked.

He knew this was one of those trick questions adults try to get past their children, but he still gave the expected answer. "Yeah, probably," he shrugged, "actually yes, I guess so."

His mother smiled softly. "Well, we can discuss it later, go on your bike ride that seems so important. Be careful and come home before dinner."

"Thanks mom!" he exclaimed, and was already halfway out the door.

Tad Tucker pedaled slowly toward Wheeler's Pond. He did not take the more direct path, but rather one that wound around to Curling Street, and avoided the kid-worn shortcut through Mr. Jones' yard. One could easily get to Wheeler's Pond Lane from Curling Street, but it was not the most efficient way to arrive. It was however, directly in the path of the Greene household. As his luck would have it, Tad cycled by right at the same moment Patty's family was coming home from an after-church luncheon. He picked up his pace as the family car pulled into the driveway, not wanting Patty to think he was stalking her home. When he was further down the street, and away from her house, he risked looking back over his shoulder and was more than surprised to see Patty standing at the end of her driveway waving to him. Tad stopped his bike, steadied himself, and returned the gesture. She smiled and waved again, then turned to run inside her front door, stopping once more on the front porch to look in his direction and wave for a third time.

Tad continued to wave at Patty before she disappeared inside. He mused for a minute or two before he shrugged his shoulders and started back on his journey. She was probably just acting nice in front of her parents anyway, he thought. He pondered this as he rode on, thinking her expression seemed genuine, but then he and boys like him had no real idea of what lie behind the smiles of girls their age. The last time they had dealt with each other they were yelling and storming away. He rode on.

When he finally arrived at Wheeler's Pond, he rode off the main road and onto a dirt feeder lane running parallel to Cooper's Ditch. There he easily retraced his former exploration back to the spot he and Luke had formerly crossed over on a wooden makeshift bridge. Sadly, he now remembered destroying this option. The current of the ditch was slowed since his last visit, and he eventually discovered another way across further up the lane. He rode back to the spot of his sighting, let his bike fall to the ground, and stood there looking at the patch of brush. He turned back to the road to gauge the distance from the car window to where he now stood. Really no more than one-hundred feet or so, he surmised. He began to search around, for what, he did not know.

He looked for anything that he could have mistaken for what he thought he saw. However, there was no debris to be found, as the park generally did a great job keeping the area litter free. He parted the grass in the exact place he found the shoe, sadly realizing he had thrown it further than its original location. There were no other signs present, and he remembered just how hard it had been raining on that day. He double-checked the area, especially where he thought he remembered flinging the shoe in frustration. The grass along the ditch bank was reedy and thick, and he eventually gave up without having any luck of locating anything other than an insect or two.

He lingered for a long time, just staring at the exact spot, occasionally scanning the entire area, and eventually meandering back to his bike. He looked behind one last time before pedaling back toward home. Tad Tucker convinced himself he had seen something that day. His coincidental discovery of a shoe in the exact same spot where he saw a little old man wearing similar shoes was just too much to overlook. Why had he thrown it away? He should have had it tested somehow. Though, he thought, any adult capable of running tests like that would have never believed him and wasted their time.

"I guess I will never know," he said out loud to himself, "I wish it had never happened." With that he pushed himself forward on his pedal and raced off down the dirt path back around to Wheeler's Pond Lane, and eventually in the direction of home. As he rode back around the site, he resisted the opportunity to look over one last time.

Had Tad Tucker looked, he may have noticed the reedy brush he had just been searching through begin to part, and five small figures emerge into the clearing. The Faeries had traveled through the night to arrive at this point hours earlier and await daylight. They had journeyed uneventfully across the human landscape in almost total silence. Even BeBoo Pevin had not talked during their trek, as they all equally felt the despondency emitting from Pedwyn Dale. They knew with their mission having been a failure, Pedwyn Dale would face the wrath of the King of Hollow Hill, and the Shee-Queen would not be able to help him. Her solution had been an easy one, but still they failed. Pedwyn Dale would now be subject to potential banishment to any various awful place, or look forward to an unbearable amount of time within the Shale. Fee the Dink had not cooed or buzzed in the slightest on their way back to Wheeler's Pond. Even Wippa had managed to give sympathetic looks toward Pedwyn. To blame the Bogie was unfair, and Pedwyn had unselfishly told them all so the night before. His was the appointed leadership of the party, and therefore, he should have known that letting Hetchy hold onto anything even remotely edible and expecting him not to eat it, was sheer lunacy. The only talking any of them did on the prior night's journey was to constantly remind Hetchy who they were, and where they were going, and why. Ultimately, as long as he had food along the way, he seemed to not care about any of it.

Pedwyn was reflecting on all of this, knowing that each step closer to the original spot he was seen from would be one

187

step closer to the Mist-hole and his ultimate confrontation with the Elders of Faerie, who would decide his fate. He watched the Tucker one last time, finding it impossible to blame any of this on the boy either.

"Why does he keep coming here, Pedwyn?" BeBoo finally asked.

"Well friend, if I am to believe the Grey Elf, and the warnings of our Elders, he is drawn by his curiosity to Faerie and what lies beyond. This is the inquisitiveness of his kind, of men, and their longing to know more, and expose more. This is the very reason we have our laws in place. He is a young child, but I fear he will continue to be drawn here, pulled over the years by a desire to be sure, to know everything. And eventually, that could lead to him discovering the Mist-holes and well...I would be to blame for that. I should have been more careful."

"But it's not fair, Pedwyn!" BeBoo cried, stamping his feet and wanting to go back.

"Be still and easy, my little one," Pedwyn said calmly, 'the good news for you is that we are going home soon. You will be dancing in the green fields and casting cantrips again in no time."

"But it won't be the same, Pedwyn," BeBoo declared.

"No. No my little friend, it will not be," Pedwyn said patting his head lightly.

24

Tad Tucker hesitantly pulled into Luke Monroe's driveway. His winding journey back home was spent in self-reflection and inner turmoil. He knew he saw something; he also knew he could not prove it, and he knew he made a fool of himself trying to do that very thing in school, and with his family. While he also realized it was possible that he never saw a thing, the shoe kept reminding him he had to have seen something. He thought back to a week ago when he first told Luke, and how his friend was the only one so far who had accepted his story, and who had come with him to find out more. He lamented how things had turned out between them, and the message Luke had left with his father inspired him to finally attempt once again to break the ice. He knocked on the door.

Back at Wheeler's Pond, the Faerie troop had spent almost an hour in silence waiting in the spot Pedwyn had selected. They were there in anticipation of the Mist-hole randomly appearing to return them to Faerie, where Pedwyn would await sentencing. Saddened and exasperated by their failed endeavor, none of the others knew how to comfort their friend in this moment. Near the same time Tad Tucker was knocking on Luke Monroe's door, a small circle of energy began to spin and form within the air above the marshy ground near Cooper's Ditch.

"Oh hello, Tad," Mrs. Monroe greeted, "wait here, I'll get Luke." She called for her son who appeared at the door

189

seconds later. He closed it behind his mother and stepped out onto the front porch. He noticed Tad's flushed face, and the mud on his shoes.

"Hey!" he said, "Did you go bike riding without me? Didn't your dad tell you I called yesterday? I called again today but they said you had left already. I hoped you were coming over here."

Tad looked incredulous. "Hoped I was...?" he stammered, "Luke, I thought after everything...I mean...I have been...you know."

"Guess I don't," Luke said, "other than you went bike riding without me."

"Well, I went out to Wheeler's Pond. I just had to go one more time, you know? And I wanted to be alone, I suppose, just one last time there," he tried to explain.

"You went all the way out to Wheeler's by yourself? What do you mean one last time? We go there all the time. Anyway, so do you want to come inside? I finally used my good-grade money to buy that video game system you were wanting me to get. I am not as good as you are yet, but I am learning," Luke Monroe said with pride.

"Luke," Tad interrupted, "what are you talking about?"

"What?", Luke said, "what are you talking about what am I talking about? Dinner and video games."

"But it's a school night," Tad said emphatically.

"Tad," Luke said slowly, "what is wrong, you look sad or something, is there something you're not telling me?" Tad realized in that moment that his friend was being a bigger person than he was and pretending he did not need to apologize. While he appreciated this effort, he still felt the need to finally make amends.

"Look Luke," he said, "I just wanted to come here and say I was sorry, OK. I am sorry I got us laughed at and picked on more than usual. Sorry I got us in trouble at school, and the whole test stuff, and I appreciate the invitation to dinner but I'm sure you want to go study for some other Algebra thing, right? So, look man, I'm sorry, and I hope we can be good again soon."

With that, he turned and walked down the stairs and picked up his bike. Luke followed him to the edge of the front step.

"Tad," he said softly, though his friend pretended not to hear and pedaled off, "Tad, wait up, seriously...Tad!" But his friend was frantically cycling back down the street, his image fading smaller as time and distance carried him farther away.

Luke stood there in the dwindling half-light and watched his friend turn the corner out of view. For some reason he kept watching for a few seconds longer just to make sure. As he was about to re-enter his home, he turned one last time to where Tad had vanished and stared.

"What's Algebra?" he said to himself, then thought little else of it, and returned inside.

25

Fee the Dink was the first one through. As soon as the Mist-hole began to appear the Faeries knew they had to be quick. Instead of waiting for the entire hole to emerge, Fee took the opportunity to fly into it as it was just her right size. They all instantly realized this was the correct plan. Since they had not been overly talkative prior to now, they had not bothered to formulate any strategy for properly jumping into a Mist-hole. In fact, only Pedwyn Dale had previously ever done so. BeBoo Pevin was next, and the Pixie wasted little time darting into the expanding hole, followed by Wippa, Hetchy, and finally Pedwyn. Pedwyn Dale took one last lingering look around him. He checked to make sure both his shoes were securely on his feet, before jumping up into the shrinking portal.

They had never actually planned for where the Mist-hole would dispel them once they returned to Faerie. Most of them, excluding Pedwyn, were so excited to go to the World, the part about coming back was never properly discussed. If asked, they would have each probably guessed they would be returned to the comforts of their own beds, but this was not to be. Pedwyn Dale and his four Faerie companions found themselves floating within a twinkling yellow-amber light, and when it dissipated, they were all very unhappy to find themselves back within their dingy cell. They were back inside the Shale.

"Wait a minute," BeBoo said loudly, "this isn't fair! I thought we were exonerated!"

"You be exterminated, Pixie, just you wait," the Goblin slurred from behind, causing them all to whirl around. He said this to scare BeBoo, but JubJub knew full well no one was going to be exterminated today.

"Jubs!" BeBoo yelled, "It's good to see you again, you handsome fellow." The Pixie was instantly falling back into his old tricks. The Goblin approached the bars of their cell and clanged them with his spear.

"Pevin!" he said loudly, "me not handsome, just checked in the mirror down the hall like you say, me look like good Goblin!" he said loudly and proudly. BeBoo knew he was lying about the mirror since he had made that story up a week ago.

"Wait, you JUST checked?" BeBoo asked slower, "When did I say to check?"

"You just say me to check, Pixie Pevin!" JubJub snarled, "and I go check and me nooo not pretty boy me uggleee and good." The Goblin continued to prance and preen in the opposite way someone just confirming being unattractive would consider. BeBoo turned to the others in disbelief.

"We've been here this whole time!", he guessed, "it is like we never left."

"But that can't be, clearly we left, we were there for days, we all remember right?" Pedwyn asked. Looking around as each of them nodded their heads. When he got to the Bogie he stopped. "Well," he said, "we were definitely not here this whole time."

"How do you know for sure?" BeBoo asked.

Pedwyn scrunched his face in uncomfortable memory. "Because" he said, "the Bogie still has Mooncheese crumbs in his beard." He pointed, and they all turned to Hetchy accusingly.

"Cizi doh," the Bogie mewled, "cizi, wazz yo num?" He was beginning to slip back into Bogie-speak in the more comfortable and familiar, to him at least, surroundings of the Shale cell. BeBoo rolled his eyes at the creature and looked at Pedwyn.

"I guess you are right," the Pixie said, "but it seems we have come back to the same spot we came from." It made no sense as he said it, so he said it in a nonsensical way and left it at that. Just as he was about to issue a rejoinder, the cell began to glow in a warming, comforting, and familiar pale-yellow radiance.

The almond eyes of the Shee-Queen gazed down on the five companions. As she tenderly smiled at each of them, the bars of the cell seemed to fade away. The Shee-Queen hovered ghost-like. Her flowing dress shimmered back and forth, heating up the cool stone floors to a bearable degree. She slowly scanned the small room and made eye contact with each of them, as if reading their faces and thoughts at the same time. She eventually turned her focus onto their leader.

"Pedwyn Dale," her sing-song voice resonated in the chamber and with everyone present. This number not only included the five adventurers, the Queen's Pillywiggin entourage, and the Goblin guard, JubJub, but also his replacement, Snee, who had just arrived for his shift having no idea what he was walking into. JubJub quickly grabbed him and decided they were better off just going down the hall to check on Mik-of-the-Lob. The Shee-Queen, somehow sensing what was occurring behind her, patiently waited for the Goblins to take their leave. As her focus returned to Pedwyn Dale he felt his knees weaken and assumed his punishment was about to be revealed.

"I am so very pleased to see you, Mr. Dale, safe and returned to us whole and welcome," she sang in vocal tones which briefly calmed him and soothed the others, "I hope you were all well behaved and able to offer your assistance during this venture."

"Yeah, but he ate...!!!" BeBoo was pointing toward the Bogie, when the Shee-Queen held her arm up and hushed him. He quickly went silent.

"Hetchy of the Marrow Bog", the Shee-Queen spoke. Hetchy stopped picking up parts of the floor to chew on and stared up at her.

BeBoo whispered to Pedwyn, "I didn't know he was from Marrow Bog, did you Pedwyn? Now I feel bad."

"Why?" Pedwyn asked, "the Bogies actually like living at Marrow Bog?"

"They do?! Ewww," BeBoo said back, before Pedwyn hushed him again.

"Come before me, little one," the Shee-Queen continued, motioning the Bogie forward. "You may leave now Hetchy, may your Bog run cold and deep," she used the traditional Bogie farewell in a way that made Hetchy swell up. He bowed low and proud, then departed the cell. He turned back to look at his companions who were waiting for him to issue some form of apology or condolences, but he simply shrugged his shoulders in a way that said he did not even know what he was there for in the first place. Hetchy the Bogie then exited the Shale.

"My sweet Fee," the Shee-Queen called, "may I speak with you close?" Fee the Dink wasted no time flying up toward the Queen's face. The floating Pillywiggins fluttered away and gave her room. The Shee-Queen began to sing in a shrill chirping vocal that echoed the Dink language and Fee chittered and buzzed about in a very clear ecstatic state.

"That sounds lovely, Miss Fee, I shall very much look forward to it. Give them all my best," the Shee-Queen said in her own voice. Fee ballooned up and let out a bursting chirp which caused the Queen to giggle with glee as the Pillywiggins all fluttered about, confused by the outburst. Fee the Dink then flew down to Pedwyn Dale. She landed at his feet, looking up at him with the only expression of sadness she could muster, which still caused him to smile.

"Goodbye to you too, Miss Fee," Pedwyn said through welling tears, "it has been a most splendid journey, and we would all have been poorer without your company. May you fly with the wind and land in the heather." She flew up and kissed Pedwyn on the cheek, then kissed the rest of them, which they all allowed, even Wippa. With that, Fee the Dink flew out of the dark damp walls of the Shale and back to the honey-soaked home she longed for and missed.

Pedwyn Dale looked forlorn and nervous as his friends began to dwindle. It was becoming clear to him how the Shee-Queen was not holding any of his companions accountable for the failure of their mission. He knew the fault deservedly lie with him, and ultimately, she would reveal his fate. The Queen seemed to notice his shifting nervous stance and smiled at him in a way that both warmed him and confused him.

"Whippatha, He that Stalks and Steals," the Shee-Queen said in a very serious voice, denoting the significant nature of the title earned by their companion. Wippa slinked forward with his head bowed low in proper deference.

"What is that all about?" BeBoo whispered to Pedwyn, who shrugged his shoulders. "Some Spriggan thing I guess,"

BeBoo ascertained. Pedwyn simply nodded, sensing his time was nearer.

The Shee-Queen put her hand down and touched Wippa on the shoulder. The Spriggan did not flinch. "Next time," her voice echoed, "you need not spare me from your pranks. I can take care of myself," she smiled. Wippa nodded in acknowledgment, but still knew he would never put a prickle-thorn in any seat of the Shee-Queen. "You have earned your release my little one, may you go and find what others have not yet realized they have lost," she said nobly.

Pedwyn realized the Shee-Queen was well adept at the verbiage of her constituency. The Spriggans loved to excuse themselves from thievery by having a clever saying which somehow always blamed the victim. Wippa turned to go, but he paused and looked back. He let his eyes meet those of both Pedwyn Dale and BeBoo Pevin. They lingered there on each of them, and he gave them each a simple and very honest nod of respect. They both realized the enormity of such a gesture and could not help but instantly miss their Spriggan friend as he turned and crawled low out of the Shale and off toward home, and a well-deserved rest.

The Shee-Queen looked down at the two remaining Faeries and smiled. They both looked up at her, then at themselves, and realized she was saving the best, or undoubtedly in their cases, the worst, for last. They both looked extremely nervous in the agonizing seconds it took before she spoke once more.

"BeBoo Pevin, Medium of the Hill Pixen, Gardner of the King of Hollow Hill, please step forward," she tried to sound sincere but broke up a little laughing to herself how BeBoo took neither of his job titles very seriously. She stared down at him a little longer than she need to, feeling a bit guilty at making him suffer somewhat, but the Pixie needed a confidence adjustment. "You have been a gift to us all my magical one," BeBoo was already surprised at where this was going as the Shee-Queen continued, "your powers of magic and insight have been a blessing BeBoo Pevin, but your greatest magic has always been your kindness, and the caring friendship you bring to others. Pedwyn Dale could not have been luckier that you were his companion on this quest." As she said this BeBoo beamed and turned to Pedwyn who had started to shake his head in complete disagreement but the look on the Pixie's face made him shift to nodding along in accord.

"Tis True, my friend," he said, "thank you for everything."

"Am I to go now your majesty?" BeBoo asked politely, correctly assuming he was not about to be in trouble.

"Yes, my little one, you too may go, go back to your green hills and never take anything seriously until it seriously tries to take you." Again the Shee-Queen knew the exact nuisance of particular Pixen logic. "And BeBoo," she continued, smiling, "While I loved the flowers you grew for me, on the event of my next journey here, I think I should like them in their natural state."

BeBoo smiled and bowed low. "Oh, I think I shall resign as Gardner, my Queen, in order to concentrate on my Spell-Craft. I think the King would be better off hiring someone with a green thumb."

"But you literally have green thumbs," Pedwyn spoke from behind, pointing out the obvious.

"Oh hush up, Pedwyn," BeBoo said with scorn, before realizing this might be the last time he would ever playfully argue with his friend. He looked up at the Shee-Queen with a pitched plea expression. He then ran over to Pedwyn Dale and hugged him tight. Pedwyn was taken aback but returned the embrace warmly.

"I'm sorry for everything, Pedwyn," BeBoo sighed, "I should have done more."

"You did all you could do, BeBoo," Pedwyn said softly, "and I shall never forget it, or you, even on the Nil Fields I will laugh at your antics."

BeBoo wiped tears from his minty-green face and declared factually, "You can't laugh on the Nil Fields, Pedwyn."

"Yes, I know this! I was just trying to be nice, never mind then, Goodness me!" Pedwyn started to argue with the Pixie, but saw BeBoo smiling and knew he had riled him up one last time just for fun. "Ahh, Mr. Pevin," Pedwyn smiled, "go now my friend, and know that I shall take your memory to whatever field I have to."

BeBoo turned to the Shee-Queen with tears streaking his small face. "Please your majesty, please don't banish Pedwyn Dale, or please don't let the King do it either. He is a good soul, he didn't mean to be seen, he's just clumsy, and lazy, and really lazy and..." Pedwyn rolled his eyes from behind as the Shee-Queen tried not to laugh. "...and he's my best friend," BeBoo concluded. Pedwyn realized his own face was by then streaked with tears as well.

BeBoo Pevin slowly and quietly left the cell, walked down the hallway towards the exit and peered from beneath his deer-skin cap. "Goodbye Pedwyn Dale, goodbye, and thank you for letting me see the World with you."

"Goodbye my friend," Pedwyn said through tears.

26

Pedwyn Dale now stood alone in front of the Shee-Queen, not counting a few Pillywiggins who flitted freely about her; though they seemed to be paying no direct attention to the seriousness of the proceedings. He watched BeBoo Pevin disappear around the corner and wiped a tear from his eye at the thought of never seeing the Pixie again. Sure, he was annoying and troublesome, but Pedwyn had never realized BeBoo considered him a best friend, and hearing him declare so made Pedwyn very proud. But still, he had to face his penalty. He turned back toward the Shee-Queen and looked up at her with all the nobility he could manage.

"So, your radiance," he used this term in a last ditch effort to make amends, "where is it that I am to be banished?" As he asked this, he winced at hearing himself even say the term, and dreaded her answer. Of all the places banishments had been carried out in the far past, none were good. Hollow Hill was a wonderful place to him and his neighbors, but there were many locations within Faerie that most should avoid. He closed his eyes in preparation for her decision.

"Are you so quick to leave your home, Pedwyn Dale?" the Shee-Queen asked with all traces of laughter and previous frivolity gone from her voice, "I have asked you this question before. I do not suspect your answer has changed, nor has mine."

"But your majesty," he stammered, "my mission was a failure. You graciously allowed me to correct my mistake, but I failed you."

"You did not fail me, Pedwyn Dale," she answered, "I am right here as I have always been. I do not feel failed in any way."

"But" he said, "I do not understand. I was seen by a human child. And I received a sentence of being seen, which means banishment. And while you provided me the means to escape my sentence, I did not accomplish this quest. So, I suppose I failed myself?"

"And do you feel failed, Pedwyn Dale?" she asked calmly. He shook his head and shrugged his shoulders.

"But I did fail in my mission, everything about it was a failure," he declared in exasperation.

"My friend," she said in a lilting soft reassuring voice, "allow me to show you what you consider failure." With that she motioned to the back wall of the Shale cell. There a shimmering image began to appear before Pedwyn, and he realized he was being shown scenes from the World.

The first image showed him and his companions on the window sill, while BeBoo hid behind the cake container. The Tucker parents slowly ate their meal in uncomfortable quiet. The image shimmered and Chuck Bain appeared, yelling at the Tucker for the fact only a single sandwich was present in his bag.

The magical image then showed Chuck eating that sandwich alone during lunch. Again the wall blurred, and Luke Monroe was wrapping up another sandwich Tad had not eaten, saving it for his bike ride home, sitting alone on a park bench absentmindedly eating the snack while studying his books. The image shimmered once more, and Tad Tucker was letting Patty Greene take his last slice of pizza, which Wippa had...

"I do not understand any of this, My Queen," Pedwyn moaned, "all this shows is the many failures we experienced under my leadership."

"Look again, little one," the Shee-Queen spoke, "look again and you will not see failure. You will see endless and all possibilities, but you will not see failure."

Pedwyn turned back to the wall and the misty magical images continued.

The Tucker father playfully tugging at his wife's robe, her falling into his embrace. The couple reaching down next to their children and holding hands in church. Taking a day off from work to spend with each other, ignoring calls from a lawyer's office they no longer needed to hear from. Ronald Tucker bringing Helen flowers home from work. Pedwyn Dale seemed confused. Until the scene again showed the parents eating the family lasagna dinner. Pedwyn gasped.

"Ronald and Helen Tucker forgot the insignificant things they allowed to build up inside of them which caused them to overlook the reasons they originally fell in love," the Shee-Queen related, as they both watched the images shifting, "They forgot their petty troubles. They will provide their children with a wonderful stable home filled with love and kindness. This is not failure, Pedwyn Dale."

"But the Tucker..." Pedwyn stammered, as he noticed the scene shifting again.

Chuck Bain holding the door for his classmates. Chuck Bain helping Luke Monroe fix his dislodged bike chain, then inviting him to play football with his friends. Chuck offering Tad uplifting advice on his soccer game. The image shifted again, and Chuck was instructing his former bully gang to lay off Luke and the others. They saw no reason to argue. Pedwyn again looked at the Shee-Queen.

"Charles Bain forgot the reasons he was black inside. He has forgotten the worrisome happenstances that have led him to show his emotions through his physical presence. He forgot his desire to bully and threaten in order to gather attention and attract friends. He will forever be an ally and companion to both Thaddeus Tucker and Lucas Monroe. They will build memories to last past any of their recollections of former hostilities. This is not failure, Pedwyn Dale."

"Oh my, but we did not intend..." Pedwyn stuttered.

"Do not let intention stand in the path of accomplishment, Pedwyn Dale, continue to watch," the Shee-Queen instructed as the scenes on the wall shifted once again.

"Are you going to eat that?" Luke Monroe asked Tad, who allowed him to wrap his uneaten chicken sandwich and save it for later. Luke Monroe asking his parents if he could play a sport, to be a part of a team. Luke playing catch in the backyard with his father. Luke high fiving Chuck when the former bully not only fixed his bike chain for him, but taught him how to fix it himself in the future. Pedwyn watched as the scenes showed nothing but Luke smiling and playing like a typical ten-year old human male child.

"Lucas Monroe forgot to worry about tomorrow and let himself see today. His brain has not been affected by the Mooncheese power. He is still as intelligent as he has ever been. But he has forgotten the stress, his reluctance to take chances, and the labels given to him at an early age that are difficult to overcome in the human world. Lucas Monroe will play at sport, and music, and games, and excel still on his subjects of learning, but he will miss no quality time with his friends and companions, his memories will be soaked in nothing but joy as he grows and prospers. This is not failure, Pedwyn Dale.

Pedwyn begin to fight back tears as the reality of the Shee-Queen's revelation started to wash over him. The scenes on the misty wall began to shimmer once again and the girl appeared. She sat and ate the pizza slice Tad had gifted her.

Waving at Tad as he biked past her house. Silencing her gossiping friends and teaching them to not prejudge people. Cheering her friends on at their soccer games. Letting her popularity with her classmates allow her to show them all that there is goodness in all of them, uniting them with a common respect.

"Patricia Greene will forget the things she saw that embarrassed the Tucker. She will forget laughing at him, seeing him cry, and the arguments they got into as a result of these proceedings. The girl already possessed such goodness within, she will now not be limited to who she shares that goodness with. She will be a steady beacon of friendship and light for all who know her. She has forgotten to be anything otherwise. This is not failure, Pedwyn Dale."

"Will the Tucker and the Greene girl ever..." Pedwyn asked, realizing the Shee-Queen was projecting future events into some of these images, and his curiosity needed to be quelled.

The Shee-Queen forced a smile, "Oh my friend, I am afraid that while the Mooncheese is a powerful magic, it causes one to forget things they no longer need know, not create in them new feelings, those have to come naturally. No matter how potent the magic is, it is not as powerful as love. Besides, she smiled, the children are too young for such things now, but perhaps seeds have been sown." She smiled in a way that hinted to Pedwyn she knew more than she was telling. "But my friend, my wonderful friend, none of this has been failure. You have gifted this child in ways that my magic, or the magic of our kind, could have never imagined on our own. Only you could have accomplished this Pedwyn Dale, it was a truly magical journey, and the Tucker's sighting of you was beyond any doubt the best thing that could have ever happened to him. There is just one lingering concern, Pedwyn Dale."

"What is it your Majesty," Pedwyn wondered, hoping against hope that all this meant he was not going to be banished after all.

The Shee-Queen pointed toward the wall, one last image began to show itself and morph into others. Tad Tucker riding his bicycle home slowly and alone. Him being so down and depressed and questioning his own sanity that he failed to see his parents changing mood or his friends shifting personalities. His life was improving all around him, and yet in his view, it was all spiraling downward.

"His sighting of you changed his life for the better by far, Pedwyn Dale," she spoke, "he is just completely unaware of this fact. He will continue to be plagued with self-doubt and uncertainty. He will be haunted by the memories and be unable to accept the changes. You have to solve this my friend, there is no one now to help you, it is your task alone.

"But there is no more Mooncheese," Pedwyn stated, unsure of how to accomplish this new burden.

"Find a way, Pedwyn Dale," the Shee-Queen said, as unexpectedly she began to fade. "I will put my trust in you: Pedwyn Dale, Gatherer of Elderberries, Stalwart Adventurer, and Brave Friend." With that Pedwyn Dale realized it was not the walls of the Shale, or the Shee-Queen, who was slowly fading away; it was him.

27

For the second time in each of their lives, Tad Tucker and Pedwyn Dale met eyes. To say he was surprised to appear through a Mist-hole, suddenly and magically, at the foot of the Tucker's bed was an understatement. Pedwyn Dale nearly wet himself. Tad Tucker nearly did the same. He was sitting in his bed, reading the latest issue of his favorite comic book, when a puff of honey-smelling air caused him to look down over the top of the page. And there was the little man. Time seemed to still itself for lingering seconds as each of them feared to blink.

Finally taking leadership as the elder of the two, the little man managed to speak. "I guess you cleaned that sock out from under your bed?" he reported. With that he doffed his fading red cap and bowed low. "Pedwyn Dale at your..."

"MOM!!!!" Tad Tucker screamed. Pedwyn threw up his hands in a pleading effort to quiet the boy. Tad could sense in the desperation on the fellow's face how his mother seeing him would not be a good thing. Somehow in that moment, Tad understood.

Helen Tucker threw open the door in a rush. "Tad!", she yelled, "what's wrong?!" Tad looked towards the little man, but he was nowhere to be seen nor was the honey-smelling smoky hole in the air. He remembered the look on the man's face and quickly redirected.

"Um, did you remember to pack my lunch for tomorrow?" he asked innocently. His mother just stared at him in disbelief.

"You yelled at me about that?!" she said, "Do not do that again! You scared me half to death. Of course I packed your lunch, now turn out this light soon and go to bed, goodnight, Tad!"

"Goodnight mom, sorry, and thank you," he deflected, his entire body buzzing in excitement at realizing he was right all along!

When she shut the door Tad sat up in bed and whispered, "Are you there?"

"That I am," Pedwyn Dale said, as he emerged from beneath the covers at Tad's feet, where he had thankfully quickly hidden. "Please my friend Tucker, please do not yell out like that again," he pleaded.

"I won't, sorry about that, it's just...I mean...so, you ARE real?" Tad asked in continuing disbelief. He was sitting up straight now and staring at every single detail, his memory returning to that spot at Wheeler's Pond a week ago, this was the same man wearing the same clothes. He was not crazy. He had been right from the start! "You said your name was...?" he asked again.

"Pedwyn Dale, pleased to meet you, the Tucker," Pedwyn again bowed low.

"My name is Tad, I'm not THE Tucker, just A Tucker," the boy corrected, "And I cannot believe this! I knew I saw you that day! I told everyone, but no one would believe me! Now they are all going to be sorry! I am going to show you to everyone, my parents, my sister, my dumb friends at school, my teacher, the Principal, Chuck Dumb Face Bain, Luke, Patty, those snotty Dowdy girls, I cannot wait!" Pedwyn waited for the Tucker's rather long list to dwindle down before he threw up his hands in exasperation.

"Goodness me indeed!" he breathed, "A Tucker you cannot do those things, I must treat with you, I must ask of you something you will not want to grant me, but I beg it of you, for both of our sakes."

"It's TAD, Tad Tucker, my name is Tad, it's short for Thaddeus, but I hate that name and the kids at school all tease me, but they won't be doing that anymore after this," he continued to express the utter glee he was feeling as Pedwyn buried his head in his hands and again held up his arms to stop him.

"Tad Tucker, please, I beg you," Pedwyn pleaded, "I beg you to listen."

Tad Tucker listened. Despite every nerve in his body screaming at him to call Luke right then, to yell for his parents or sister, or even briefly he thought of snatching up Pedwyn Dale and stuffing him in a box. But despite all of those thoughts, he listened, Tad Tucker listened as Pedwyn Dale told him everything.

28

It was hours later before Pedwyn had finished, but Tad Tucker stayed awake and alert through all of it. He was mesmerized by hearing about Faerie, the reality of mermaids and unicorns, and the many details Pedwyn Dale gifted him to know. Tad Tucker became the first human in recorded history to learn this much about Faerie without suffering some horrible exchange of payment for the knowledge. Pedwyn told him how long ago the Fae would invite humans to dance with them within the mushroom ring, and tell them stories of their histories and customs. When the unsuspecting people left this revelry, they were horrified to learn they had unnaturally aged seven years. Tad only aged a couple of hours as Pedwyn told him about his home, his job, the elderberries, the King of Hollow Hill's party, his falling through the Mist-hole, and their attempts to get him to eat the Mooncheese in every way possible. Pedwyn left out the details of who had consumed the cheese, and the changes it brought about, for fear of Tad dispelling the magic by reminding the people involved of their past personality flaws. But Pedwyn Dale felt he had told Tad Tucker enough.

He leaned back on the pillow Tad provided and finished his tale, hopefully having made his point clear. Tad Tucker sat quietly for a moment before he finally spoke.

"So then, I can't tell anyone at all, any of this, for the rest of my life?" he asked dejectedly.

Pedwyn Dale nodded. "My friend Tucker, I have no more Mooncheese to force into you. I possess no malevolent magic to bind your will, and I have no trickster charms to fool you with. I was told to find a way by my Queen. I did not know I would be able to do that, but I think I have thought of a form of magic that might work."

"What kind is it?" Tad Tucker asked.

"Friendship and trust, Tad Tucker," Pedwyn said softly, "We are friends now you and I, and I have told you that I need your friendship and your trust, or I could face severe consequences, and I have hinted to you that the undoing of our trust could spell ruin for you as well. So we must trust each other to bind our friendship and mutual needs."

"This sounds like grown-up talk that I don't realize I'm getting tricked by," Tad said.

Pedwyn laughed lightly, "No friend Tucker, no trickery remember, though you are lucky some of the other fellows I know were not the ones you saw that day instead. No, I just need one thing from you to bind our trust together. It is rather simple. I need your promise."

"My promise? Like a cross my heart and hope to die kind of promise?" Tad asked back.

"Goodness me! No one should hope to die!" Pedwyn said excitedly.

"No, it's just a phrase us humans have, it doesn't mean anything, no one means it when they say that" Tad explained.

"Well," Pedwyn responded, "I need a promise that you actually do mean."

"So let me get this straight," Tad came back, "all you need is for me to promise that I will never talk about this to anyone, ever? That if anyone asks, I will say I made it all up, that it was not true, that I didn't see a thing, that I never saw an Elf."

"Yes, about that, for the um, well, for the record," Pedwyn stammered, "Um, I am not an actual Elf, I am just a, Pedwyn Dale."

"Oh, I know," Tad responded.

"You do?" Pedwyn asked.

"Yes," Tad answered, "as soon as I got an actual close up look at you, I knew you couldn't be an Elf. I mean I read the Hobbit, well, my mom read a lot of it out loud to me, and...yeah, no Elf."

"Hmmpf," Pedwyn snorted, "not sure what a Hob-Bat is but I am often confused for an Elf in my village, sometimes," he exaggerated.

"Are you really?" Tad asked skeptically.

"Well, there is this one near-sighted Greenie who lives on the hill over from me, and one time he thought I was the Elf that passes through and inspects the flower heights and...you know what, never mind this, I can appear rather Elvish at times is my point," Pedwyn finished.

Tad Tucker burst into a muffled snicker, and Pedwyn tried to maintain his stance, but eventually joined him in laughter. Together the two rolled on the bed and giggled as silently as they could manage for several minutes.

"Ahh, Mr. Tucker," Pedwyn said still chuckling, "tis a fine thing to laugh with a friend."

29

The Mist-hole expelled Pedwyn Dale to his front door. He turned and saw many of his friends and neighbors out gathering their things and going about their mornings. Even his snobby Sprite neighbor managed a polite wave, though he would later gossip that Pedwyn was actually missing a shoe buckle, which was unthinkable. Pedwyn smiled and managed a deep breath before entering his home. Everything was just as he left it and he made himself a simple meal. He realized this was the first time he was ever planning to eat a breakfast and then get into bed. But to bed was just where he planned to go, no one had better need any elderberries anytime soon. Pedwyn Dale needed to sleep for days.

After his meal, he kicked off his shoes and realized it was sadly way past time to wash his socks, but that could wait. He tucked himself into the comfort of his warm bed and tried to drift off to sleep, but his thoughts were scrambling back to the scene hours before in the World.

Tad Tucker had made his promise. He swore to Pedwyn on their friendship that he would never tell anyone about what he saw ever again. That he would never talk about any of it to anyone, ever. Pedwyn understood how difficult this would be for the child and felt even worse when the Tucker had pleaded with him to visit from time to time. Pedwyn told him of the dangers of travel to the human world and ultimately of the differing time structures between the Mists and the World. Tad had broken down when he realized it meant he would never see Pedwyn Dale again and pleaded with him to provide some lasting memory. Pedwyn had thought long and hard and had finally given him something to remember him by, a worn tarnished brass buckle from the same shoe he had lost before. Pedwyn Dale drifted off to sleep, content in the belief that his human friend would hold true to his word, and that his snooty Sprite neighbor would just have to deal with the fact he would never replace his missing buckle.

30

Tad Tucker woke that morning after getting few hours of sleep the night before, for obvious reasons. He dressed and joined his family for breakfast, which was as enjoyable and carefree as he had experienced in some time. He grabbed his lunch, kissed his mother, hugged his dad, and even gave his sister a nudge as he exited through the garage door, hopped on his bike, and made his way to Southern Shores Middle School. Halfway there Luke Monroe and Chuck Bain sped by on their bikes, surprising Tad from behind.

"Race you to school, Tucker!" Chuck said as he sped by, "last one there is a rotten egg!" Tad was not about to earn that slander and was just about to increase his speed, when he heard another bike rider approaching again from behind.

"Hey Tad!" Patty Greene said as she passed him slowly "want to ride to school with me?" she inquired. He turned to watch the boys speeding off and looked at her.

"Sure," he said, "I'll be a rotten egg then." Patty smiled, misunderstanding the statement and they talked all the way to class.

The school day passed wonderfully for Tad Tucker, the actions of Luke and Chuck, and Patty, and really all the others, seemed to sweep him up into a network of friends and fun, mixed with actual learning too. He sat with his friends at lunch, he had no worry to avoid Chuck anymore, and actually found him and his friends to be funny. He and Luke made plans to go stay in the tree house that weekend and Chuck asked if he could come too. Tad was caught up in an entirely new experience at school, and it was wonderful. Only on the way home did it all catch up with him when he realized how badly he wanted to tell someone about Pedwyn Dale and how it was only one day into his promise, and he was already struggling.

All his friends bicycled home together, splitting up at their respective streets and continuing on. Tad eventually made it home, and realized what a special day it had been. Still, he so wanted to tell someone about his secret. Maybe he could just drop a lot of hints until they guessed? That way, he would not have actually told them and broken his promise. He knew this was not right however, and he fumbled in his pocked for what he had placed there in the morning. Reaching out he opened his hand to show himself the little buckle. An untidy reminder to a tidy promise is what Pedwyn had said about it. Tad had laughed then at that, but the seriousness of it was now reaching him. He had to keep this promise, but it was not going to be easy. Just then the phone rang. Tad answered, and was excited to hear Luke's voice on the other line.

"What? Football? Now? In your yard? Chuck too? OK wow, yeah, um, I just got home so let me grab a snack and I'll be right over! Hey Luke? You and me on the same team, OK? Yeah! See you soon!" Tad hung up, and raced to change into his football playing clothes recalling how he had gotten in trouble last time for not avoiding grass stains on a white sweater.

224

He came down ready to play, but remembered he needed an after-school snack. He opened the refrigerator to find something quick to grab. It was there he saw the leftovers. He pulled the tray out and sat it on the kitchen table as Pedwyn's entire story came back into his head. He peeled off the cover and looked. A portion of the family meal from that night still remained inside the dish. Tad pulled out the little brass buckle from his pocket and studied it for several seconds, then he glanced back at the lasagna.

"A promise to a friend," he said softly, and retrieved a fork from the utensil drawer. He did not even bother to risk heating it up, not knowing the affects modern technology would have on Faerie magic. Tad Tucker placed the buckle back in his pocket, unsure of if the next time he found it there he would know what it was or where it was from. Tears began to well in his eyes when he realized what he was about to do. But he understood who, and what, he was going to do it for. Without further hesitation, Tad Tucker cleaned the entire plate.

He put his dishes in the sink, washed the food down with a quick glass of water, and waited. He had no idea how long the effect would take, but for now he was still aware of everything. He wiped a tear from his eye and steadied himself.

Opening the front door, Tad Tucker jumped on his bike and began to ride to his best friend's house to play football with their growing group of playmates, it was a joyous time in his young life, and a brief fog lifted as he picked up speed and raced to Luke's front yard.

It cannot be measured to the exact moment of occurrence, but somewhere along the way, Tad Tucker willingly gave up the beauty and wonders of the world of Faerie, and returned instead to the magic that is childhood.

Acknowledgements

My mother Phyllis, read *The Hobbit* out loud to me before bed each night, which eventually led to her starting, and me finishing, Tolkien's *Lord of the Rings* by the time I was in the fifth grade. She bought the 1976 Tolkien Calendar with artwork by the Brothers Hildebrandt, and I was transfixed. Friends through the years played Dungeons and Dragons with me, furthering my fascination with mythical creatures and adventure. My sister Jennifer checked out (and never returned) *Faeries* by Brian Froud and Alan Lee, and any overdue library fines still owed, would be money well spent compared to the value I have gained from that amazing tome. I began to collect every book I could on Fae lore and even wrote a grad school paper on the belief in the Little People which was still very much alive only a generation or so ago in areas such as the United Kingdom. But it was again a gift passed down from my mother, the *Giant Golden Book of Elves and Fairies*, that got this whole thing started. Thank you, mom, Professor Tolkien, Terry Brooks, and to all my family and friends that fanned and fueled and or tolerated me often escaping into the world of fantasy.

Being able to share the story of Pedwyn Dale and his companions would not have been the same without the ability to offer you glimpses into the world I have attempted to describe. I cannot thank Mark Wayne Russell enough for his amazing skill to take from my roughly outlined imagination and create the imagery on the cover and throughout this book. I felt like he introduced me to my own characters, and I will forever be grateful.

Thanks also to Paul Russell for his artistic computer skills, the logo, and visual ideas. Thank you, Chris Lowe, for your editing eye; any mistakes still remaining are clearly the result of Spriggandry. To the many readers and listeners over the long years this book was coming together. Some of you were there with me all the way, you helped me to finish what I started, thank you all.

Thank you, Tabitha, for pushing me to tie knots in all the loose strings of my many dream projects; finishing a book or two seems small compared to what you deal with daily. Your inspiration has been an undeniable boon.

In the end it seems silly to thank everyone like I have won some award or accomplished some daring feat. I came up with a nice little story in my head, talked about it for years, and finally wrote it down. Thank you, the readers, for making it all worth the while.

May your bogs run cold and deep....